DEUS EX MACHINA

An imprint from *Relentless Endeavor Press,*

Courtesy of Lulu.com, Publisher

ISBN: 978-1847283429

Second Revised Edition – 2007

Deus Ex Machina

A Comedy About Second Chances
And Divine Intervention

An Amusement Tale
by Maria Aragon

A Word:

To those who've provided me with moral support,

especially my Mother: Thanks.

To those I do not know who've bought a copy of this

work: Thanks for taking a chance on me. I hope you enjoy

it and please, tell a friend.

Sincerely,

Maria Aragon

CONTENTS:

1. Omens And Other Signs

Stewart Dunk should have known what was coming.

There had been a plague of omens, signs, warnings actually, for a week before THEY descended upon the derelict hovel next door. Still, it wouldn't have made any difference to Stewart whether he had recognized the nagging omens for what they were. There was no place he could have run to, and frankly, it would have been pointless even to try.

Monday morning at the British Museum, the first divine sigil waited in all of its ancient glory quite brazenly where the torque he had been cleaning and restoring should have been. For a long moment Stewart stared at it, a small bronze figure of the goddess Venus that he knew belonged in a display case in Room 22. Naturally, he saw to it personally that she was returned at once to where she belonged only to discover the torque sitting in her place and an alarmed curator gawking at it. A swap was made: the gold torque for the little bronze Venus, and great sighs of relief were heaved. Stewart and the curator went their separate ways, swearing to get to the bottom of it.

Tuesday morning came. Again, the torque went missing. In its place rested a bronze Corinthian helmet and when he lifted it, he found a spear point and a small Roman bronze statuette of the god Mars that belonged in the King's Library. Naturally, when he checked, his torque sat perched in place of the statuette and under the scrutiny of yet another colleague, who stood in alarmed silence before the unlocked case. They swapped objects and, muttering ominous words about pranksters, thieves, and the police, and swearing oaths of vengeance on whoever was responsible, they went their separate ways.

Wednesday morning it rained, and Stewart wasn't at all surprised to find a small Roman bronze figurine of the trickster god Mercury in the midst of the coin hoard he was to begin work on. Stewart sighed, grinned, shook his head, and returned Mercury to its case in Room 22, where the same grateful curator stood wringing his hands before an empty space in a case. Stewart spent the rest of his work hours beginning the laborious process of cleaning and preparing the coins for more intensive examination. All the while, as though a door had been left ajar, he felt surrounded by something akin to a draft. It did not leave him cold though, but strangely invigorated and if not uneasy, then restless with unfocused anticipation.

Thursday morning it surprised him not at all to find two Greek coins square in the middle of the Anglo Saxon hoard – a silver stater from Corinth with the goddess Athena's head on one side and Pegasus on the other, and a silver tetradrachm from Athens with Athena again on one side and an owl on the opposing side. You couldn't miss them. They sat in the base of a bowl from Corinth that had a Gorgon's head dead center in it. Although he wasn't surprised anymore, Stewart was sensibly alarmed, enough so that he took them directly back where they belonged.

By then a sense of consternation and moderately stifled panic had set in at the British Museum. The security cameras had revealed nothing and yet objects were popping up out of place right and left. Guards and curators muttered about hearing disembodied voices echoing amongst the statues when the museum was closed, and although they were reluctant to admit it, some of the guards swore that they felt eyes watching them whenever they passed among the Greek and Roman artifacts and statues. Stern memos from on high popped up. Vigilance became the order of the day, which was kind of redundant where the already paranoid guards were concerned. Still, they figured that someone had to be behind all of the strangeness.

Actually, from the moment Stewart arrived at work that Thursday, he felt it: a constant, percolating energy. He thought it was just him. His demanding mother had been on one of her tirades the night before because one of her dates hadn't worked out and then that morning her clothes screamed even louder than she had. He knew what that meant. She would be going out after someone's husband that evening. She would be going out, thank God. Now, if his older brothers Aiken and Erian would bugger off, Stewart might have a decent evening all to himself for a change. If he had thought it all strictly in his head or that he was the only one feeling that things were more than a little off-kilter that morning, his colleagues soon nipped that misperception in the bud.

His colleague Byron complained that he couldn't get a particularly annoying pop song out of his head. Stewart made the mistake of asking him which one and, as soon as Byron told him, had it stuck in his head too: some obnoxious cover version of a much better song from the sixties. All Stewart heard for a full hour was something about a goddess on a mountain top whose name was Venus. It took a dose of the Clash for a solid hour to clear that muck out.

After a coffee break, Stewart returned to find a Roman picture plate, a silver platter to be precise, sitting atop his hoard. Although he recognized the forms of Artemis and Athena on the plate, the figure that captured his attention though was that of Apollo holding his bow, with his lyre at his feet where he stood in a shrine. Stewart recognized also that the Roman plate would be wanted desperately elsewhere, so he returned it to its proper place. Naturally, he answered more than a few questions, shrugging all the while and tugging at his ear in consternation.

Fortunately, the security tapes vindicated him. One moment, the object had gleamed in its display case and the next it had vanished. Once again, a secure object had taken a little stroll utterly on its own.

Exchanging bemused shrugs with Byron, Stewart resumed work on the hoard.

There were no further distractions until his lunch hour.

Still feeling agitated, expectant even, Stewart wolfed down his sandwich and coffee and took off into the exhibition halls. He hoped that a prolonged stroll would soothe his nerves, so, hands in pockets, he set off on a winding circuit. He wound up among the now infamously restless Greek and Roman objects.

He regretted his detour almost immediately. The atmosphere was palpably strange. Everywhere he felt eyes upon him. He felt presences pressing close and then passing by. He imagined that he saw luminous people out of the corner of his eyes, but when he looked directly saw only eager tourists in their drab mortal attire. He would have even sworn he heard voices, odd, indistinct voices that came from nowhere and belonged to no one, speaking in breathless whispers.

In Room 17, there were, happily for Stewart's nerves, only other everyday people about taking pictures of the Nereid Monument. None of them stood about for long. They were either coming from or going to the Parthenon Galleries, except for one young man, who stood only a few paces away.

At first glance, Stewart saw nothing remarkable about him. Then, donning a baseball cap, the stranger turned his way. He noticed two things immediately: the golden wings embroidered on the cap and the mischievous and unmistakably keen look of interest the young man fixed upon Stewart. Still beaming at some secret joke, the stranger tipped his cap, revealing an unruly head of brunette hair, and sauntered past him into the Parthenon Galleries. For some alarming reason, Stewart was reminded of Harpo Marx.

Naturally, Stewart moved on – in the opposite direction – back into Room 23.

Immediately, he bumped into Keyes, one of the blue-jacketed security personnel, who usually sat in the chair in the far right corner keeping an eye on the tourists.

Keyes jumped and looked at him. "Oh!" He smiled nervously at Stewart, but his glance kept reverting to the crouching figure of Venus in the center of the space. "You startled me."

Stewart glanced with him at the marble statue. "Sorry, Keyes. 'Didn't mean to scare you."

"No. No. YOU didn't scare me. Just surprised me, that's all." Then Keyes muttered as he eyed the sculpture, "I'm not scared of you."

Stewart frowned at that. "What's there to be scared of?"

Keyes looked all about them. The tourists flowed in and out of the galleries on all sides of them. He stepped back beside Stewart and leaned close. "They wouldn't be filming one of those prank shows in here, would they?"

"Not after what's been going on with the collection cases lately they sure wouldn't," said Stewart.

"You mean all those objects disappearing and reappearing, right?"

Stewart nodded. "So far nothing's gone completely missing, but you know, everyone is tense just now, especially since the security cameras haven't caught so much as the prankster's shadow."

"Have the cameras been tampered with?"

Stewart shook his head. "That's why everyone's in knots. It's a complete mystery: objects moving in and out of cases, drawers, rooms, and no one doing it. Why do you ask anyway?"

"Because that statue keeps winking at me."

"The Venus?"

Keyes nodded.

" 'Kidding, right?"

Keyes shook his head vehemently.

"Uh…that's impossible."

"I KNOW!" Keyes lowered his voice, "As clear as day, she winked at me – THREE TIMES. Three times, Stewart. She kept leering at me so much that I had to get up out of my chair and move out of her range. I swear though that she's watching me out of the corner of her eye right now. Move around to the right and watch her. You'll see."

Keeping his gaze fixed on the sculpture's face, Stewart walked deliberately around to the right. Nothing. The Venus sculpture behaved as all sculptures did and sat perfectly still.

Keyes sighed and chewed on his thumbnail.

Stewart said, carefully, "Maybe you should take a break."

"I don't think it would do any good." He retreated

a sensible if paranoid distance from the statue's backside where she couldn't turn to wink at him. He probably wouldn't be sitting in that chair in the corner again any time soon.

Stewart checked his watch and decided to leave Keyes to chew on his fingernails. His glance fell upon a man standing at the top of the steps to Room 22 where a Roman full-figured marble sculpture of the god Apollo stood. There was something so arresting about the tall stranger with the thick fiery hair that Stewart faltered in mid-turn and instinctively frowned. It wasn't just his striking appearance that snagged Stewart's attention, but also manner in which he chewed on his bottom lip, twisting his mouth to one side, and made displeased sounds.

"Please tell me," said the fire-haired man in a loud voice, "that I didn't really look like that back in the day, did I?"

Two women joined him from within Room 22. They were easily two of the most strikingly attractive women Stewart had ever seen – a blonde woman and an African beauty who kept her braids confined snug within a red bandanna. A tourist jostled the African lady.

Stewart would have sworn that he heard a snake's rattle. He glanced about, but saw only Keyes attempting to sit again in his chair unmolested. Keyes looked everywhere but at the face of the Venus that was turned past him facing the Assyrian galleries.

The two women eyed the marble statue of Apollo with its almost Rapunzel-length tresses and faced their male companion. They grinned.

"No. Oh, come on," the man complained.

Both women burst into laughter.

"Thanks a bunch, you two." The red-haired man

shoved his hands into his pockets and headed past the Apollo into Room 22.

His two companions sped after him.

"Come on, Apollo," said the blonde, "don't sulk."

"If you think you look ridiculous," said the dark lady, "come with me. There's a perfectly hideous picture of me in a bowl down this way. It looks like a bearded man sticking his tongue out." She caught his arm and steered him in the general direction of Room 13.

The blonde brought up the rear. "Actually, it looks like Ares when he's hungover."

Their male companion chuckled and glanced back at her.

Stewart averted his gaze. It landed on that rather fey-looking sculpture of Apollo up the steps.

The exotic trio veered into Room 17, where the Nereid Monument stood.

A moment later a loud voice emerged from that gallery. "No, it does not look like me!"

Both Keyes and Stewart stared as a tall man stopped in the doorway to the Nereid Monument.

"I'll remember you said that, Medusa," he added. Grumbling, he marched directly up the steps past the Apollo and into Room 22. He stopped though to take a long look at the sculpture and moved on into the room, chuckling.

Stewart exchanged looks with Keyes. A sense of excitement mingled uneasily with foreboding gripped Stewart. It wasn't entirely an apprehensive feeling, just a nagging sense once again that something was going on, or that something was about to happen. Tornado weather was said to feel just like this. Stewart glanced at his watch. It was time to get back to work.

As the afternoon progressed however, reports

trickled in. Keyes had gone home early and had been given Friday off as well. The general consensus was that Keyes was one of the truly dedicated veterans, so for him to complain that the statues were talking to him gave everyone pause.

Then when his replacement fled Room 23 too not an hour later, and his replacement refused to sit anywhere near the crouching Venus or even look at it, everyone began to wonder is there wasn't something in the water.

Stewart went home wondering what could possibly happen next.

Then Friday arrived.

2. Friday Morning: The New Neighbors

Friday morning dawned glamorous with bright spring sunshine. It did little for the drab Essex suburb with its unremarkable look-alike houses that had lost their 'new home' glamour within a week of becoming occupied sometime back in the Seventies. Confined with his mother and two older brothers, Stewart lived in a house on the corner, the one with the cherished garden gnomes, coddled roses, trimmed lawn, and unused and frankly mint condition lawn furniture. By contrast, its neighbor languished in ominous neglect. Its lawn was not only ragged, but rife with proud bright new dandelions, and until that early spring morning had been unoccupied. Every morning Stewart had gazed out at it from his bedroom window and wondered who would be brave enough to move into it. It wasn't the renovation that would require courage, but having to live next door to Stewart Dunk's mother Udela.

His mother Udela Dunk was a certifiable morning person, but that morning her condition was a little more acute than usual. It didn't help that yet again her rendezvous had gone pear-shaped when her date's wife came home early. When she was in this particular state, her words ganged up in packs, like veritable hounds from hell capable of forcing anyone to sky dive into a boiling volcano. Udela's relentless mood drove Stewart outside into the morning damp.

Provisioned with only a slice of toast in one hand

and a cup of coffee in the other, Stewart's flight stopped on the patio's edge, for God forbid he tread on the precious lawn. Surrounded only by the cool of the morning and the singing of birds, Stewart let go a sigh and cast an imploring look heavenward as he held his toast between his teeth, loosened his tie and collar, a nagging habit of anxiety. Nothing eased his misery this morning, so Stewart pulled forth a lawn chair and sat upon it as he finished his toast and coffee. With each bite and ensuing gulp, he regained a little more of his natural good-natured equilibrium. Sitting with his back to the house helped too.

The birdsong ceased – abruptly. Stewart frowned at the hedges and trees. Was Mrs. Nesbit's orange marmalade cat skulking about nearby? No, no cat, orange or otherwise, but then he heard a jaunty whistle sailing forth from the sidewalk beyond the high fence. He shifted to see who it was who could be so bloody cheerful at that hour.

As jaunty as his whistle, as bold as his martial melody, a tall, brutishly handsome man in comfortable athletic work clothes marched up to the stooping gate belonging to the house next door. In time to his melody, the stranger kicked open the gate and continued his march across the lawn and up upon the back porch. He paused to look directly at Stewart, saluted him, and without missing a beat in his Sousa march opened the back door with a single shove that would have done a footballer proud.

In he went, but briefly he poked his head back out and grinned. "Morning!"

Stewart half-waved his cup-bearing hand at him. "Morning."

The stranger withdrew into the derelict house again. The martial air resumed, accompanied by an alarming series of crashes and bangs that nearly caused Stewart to spill his coffee all over his freshly pressed clothes. Suddenly, he remembered. He had seen the same man in the Museum yesterday. He had been grousing back at someone he called 'Medusa'.

"Odd," muttered Stewart.

Udela emerged through their back door onto the patio. Due to her garishly colored attire into which she had crammed her aging voluptuousness, Stewart's mother resembled something akin to a ship's masthead. "Who was that?"

Stewart cringed as he always did. "It looks like we have a new neighbor."

"Did you get a good look at him? Was he young or older?"

"He looked like one of Aiken's drinking mates," Stewart muttered. Using pure mind power, he concentrated on willing her and her blinding clothes back into the house, but she refused to budge. Typical.

"Oh! An athletic sort. A footballer maybe?" The woman was fairly drooling.

Stewart shuddered and crunched on his toast. "Haven't you got enough conquests, Mum?"

Udela ignored his comment. She ignored most things he said. Instead, she set a plate on the table beside her youngest son.

Stewart turned away from the greasy mess.

He found himself shoved back into the lawn chair and the plate shoved into his free hand. His lip curled at its contents. His stomach churned.

If she had lingered a trifle longer, she would have seen the rebellious look Stewart took on, but she didn't. She was certain that Stewart would mind her, and in absolute certainty, had turned on her heel and returned indoors to a kitchen that rivaled its mistress in garishness.

Stewart sank into a despondent funk, his head hanging nearly between his knees. With a deep sigh, he sat up straight, and finished the last of his toast, washing it down with a deep gulp of coffee. The breakfast plate he set upon the table and pushed away as though it were radioactive waste.

"Ares! You minotaur!" came a sudden outburst. It was followed by a grumble. "Actually, the Minotaur would have done less damage."

The man inside shouted, "I heard that!"

The tall, more dashingly dressed man at the now broken gate commented lowly, "You were meant to."

Stewart gaped. He remembered this man too from the Museum yesterday. It also struck him as odd in that he had neither seen nor heard the tall, peculiarly radiant bloke arrive. Vaguely, he had noticed a brief, intense stroke of sunlight cutting through the soft morning atmosphere right before he had heard the fair-haired stranger's voice. Still, when his mother was on one of her rants, it was hard to notice anything else or to think of anything else, except escaping, even if only into the corner of one's own mind. The second stranger possessed a glance so potent and inexplicably intrusive that Stewart felt its peculiar, warm strength when it landed briefly, but tellingly upon him. Stewart rubbed his eyes and gawked in spite of himself. There was indeed a subtle, but pervasive golden aura about the man. The stranger's ill humor gave way to more naturally buoyant spirits as he tried to upright the gate. For a moment, he had it fixed, but then it tumbled down onto the overgrown grass, mashing a few dandelions in the process. Instead of cursing, he grinned.

Then two women joined the man on the sidewalk and flanked him. Like Day and Night they were, for one was as blond and as radiant as the other was earthy and dark. Easily, they were two of the most distractingly attractive women Stewart had ever seen, in his neighborhood or anywhere else for that matter. They were also the same two women from the Museum. Stewart got a weird feeling in his stomach.

The blonde wore an expression of irritation. "Great. Just great. I told you, Apollo, we should've left sooner."

His grin freezing on his face, the radiant man addressed as Apollo glanced sharply at Stewart, saying lowly, " 'Ixnay on the 'pollolay, 'thenalay." Then he said, normally. "The gate can be fixed, 'Minnie'."

"Minnie?" snapped the blonde lady.

The one she had addressed as Apollo nudged her and cast a look in Stewart's direction.

Stewart was frowning already. He knew what he had heard. Ares. Apollo.

"What? Oh." 'Minnie' smiled innocently and waved at their neighbor. "Hello there." Her patience was already strained, if one could judge by the manner in which she twisted her mouth, marring her lovely looks. Just like the one she had addressed as 'Apollo', Stewart detected a subtle aura shining from her being. The Pre-Raphaelites would have throttled one another to be the first to paint her fair features, shining eyes, and tumbling, thick golden hair.

A crash and a thud issued from the no longer neglected house.

"Lord! He's tearing up the house," cried the dark beauty from the mother continent. Her eyes glowed like amber, but turned as sharp and crisp as faceted citrines as yet another crash came from the house. Apart from her remarkable eyes, she possessed no distinctive aura, but then Stewart noticed that the gleaming black braids that she kept tightly confined by a red bandanna moved even when she did not. Was she wearing a snake on her head? Suddenly, he remembered that snake rattle he had heard in the Museum. The mental image of the redoubtable and utterly fearsome Medusa erupted forth in his mind.

'Apollo's' electric gaze remained fixed on Stewart. "Don't panic, 'Meddles'."

"Meddles?" she retorted. She narrowed her glowing eyes at him.

"Yes, MEDDLES." He nodded his head toward Stewart.

A third woman, possessed not only of the most effortless beauty Stewart had ever seen, but also a buoyant strut that would have put Marilyn Monroe to shame, strolled past them, between the gate posts, over the fallen gate, and toward the back door. Even in her eagerness to gain the sanctuary of house, she took a moment to fix a smile upon Stewart that warmed him all the way down to his toes. Smiling was something of a bad habit of which she refused to break herself. When she heard a bang and another crash from within, her smile lit up anew. "He's here! Oh good!"

"So this is your doing," said the blonde.

"Don't get your robes all knotted up, Athena. I'll see that he fixes it."

Apollo buried his face in his hands and shook it in exasperation. Then he cast a worried look at Stewart, who eyed 'Athena' with a fresh frown. He motioned warningly to the newest arrival, that beautiful creature, and gave a small meaningful glance in Stewart's direction.

Scarcely acknowledging Apollo's gesture, the beautiful one paused on the back porch and gave a world-weary sigh. "Very well. I'll fix the gate myself."

The radiant duo raised their hands. "No!"

The African beauty with the coiling hair merely shook her head violently.

"Are you sure?" said the beautiful one as sweetly as ever.

As Minnie, or Athena, nodded a little too vigorously, Apollo said, "We'll leave it for now. Hermes – er, Herman - might find it easier to come and go without the gate."

Stewart made swift note of that slip too.

"See? It all worked out for the best." The beautiful one went within.

The random thumps and crashes ceased for the time being.

"Maybe they'll get it out of their system before nightfall." 'Meddles' wrinkled her nose at the upstairs windows.

The ones named Athena and Apollo said, "No, they won't."

"I call the couch!" said Meddles before either could say another word.

"Damn it, Medusa," snapped Athena.

Medusa?! Stewart felt as though he'd been struck by a lightning bolt.

"Hey! I'm not sitting upstairs all night listening to them go at it. You two had better buy some earplugs if you want to get any sleep at all," said Medusa.

Apollo picked up the gate and propped it against the fence dividing their yard from that of the Dunk household. In that moment, he locked very firm gazes with Stewart, and as affable as ever, nodded in greeting.

Stewart nodded back.

A young man zipped past down the sidewalk. Besides his brisk, almost blurry pace, the only other distinctive thing Stewart saw was the baseball cap on the chap's unruly head and the golden wings embroidered onto it. Well, that and that keen Marxian grin the young man flashed his way.

"So, this is the new homestead?" the young man had said in passing.

Medusa called after him. "Unfortunately, yes."

He zipped past – in the opposite direction this time. "Ares got here first again, eh?"

Apollo winced and glanced again at Stewart. "Yes," he groaned.

Athena called after him. "Didn't you get the memo?"

He blurred past again. "What memo?"

"He has decided that he likes his Roman name better, so we're supposed to use that from now on." Athena rolled her eyes. "I blame his mother."

"Don't we all?" said Apollo.

At last the young chap stopped in the gateway and eyed the damage. "Don't tell me – you want me to fix this."

"That depends: will it be easier for you to come and go without the gate, Herman?" said Apollo.

"Herman?!" The young man gave him an odd look.

"Yes, HERMAN," Apollo said with particular emphasis.

He gave Apollo another odd look. "Easier, I expect."

Athena shrugged at the broken gate. "It's decided then. We leave it off."

Herman set his sights on Stewart, who had missed nothing. "That's the bloke we're supposed to help, right? Stewart Dunk."

Again, Apollo buried his face in his hands and

shook it. "A little louder please, Greenland didn't hear you."

Herman harumphed and, tilting his chin skyward, stomped off.

"Say," Stewart folded his arms across his chest, "how did you know my name?"

"I'm sorry. Introductions are in order." Apollo walked down his side of the fence until he stood directly opposite of Stewart. He extended his hand over the fence. "We wouldn't want to seem unneighborly now, would we? Minnie? Meddles?"

"God forbid," said the blonde, as she joined Apollo.

Stewart set his coffee cup aside and wiping his hands on his trousers, began to rise.

At that moment his older brothers Aiken and Erian burst out through the back door. Aiken zeroed in on Stewart's breakfast plate. Erian took one look at the three attractive strangers gazing over the fence at them and stopped to gawp.

Stewart noticed how Apollo rested his hand upon the fence and eyed his two older brothers with quiet concentration.

"Waste not, want not," Aiken grunted. He inhaled Stewart's breakfast and he was welcome to it as far as Stewart was concerned. Aiken was not only the eldest, but also the largest of the three Dunk boys. He wore his hair closely cropped and moved everywhere with a virile swagger punctuated by the supposedly, or so he thought, handsome sneer that he had adopted when he was fourteen.

Whereas Aiken was obviously all alpha male, Erian resembled the white-collar alpha he aspired to be. The smug expression he wore arose from the dead certainty that he was cleverer by far than most of the people around him. Actually, he was quite clever, but it isn't polite to be so arrogant about it now, is it? Stewart noticed how Athena's glance locked immediately upon Erian in the manner reminiscent of a lion zeroing in on the one weak gazelle in a whole herd.

Stewart wound up beside the fence, feeling oppressed more than ever by his brothers. He wished for a pair of wings to bear him away, something, anything - a rickety old Medieval Deus ex Machina that would descend from the sky and deliver him from his relations. It seemed though that no matter what he did, or how hard he thrashed about, walls stood steadfast, and doors remained shut, as though they had been bricked up on the other side. The sense of suffocation grew so intense at those moments that Stewart would breathe that much harder.

A hand reached over the fence. Stewart looked up into Apollo's smiling face and into those of Athena and Medusa, whose hair looked normal enough although her eyes made his hair stand on end.

"Let's start over," said Apollo. "My name is Pajawone, but my friends call me Phoebus."

Incredulous, Erian moved closer. "Pajawone? Phoebus? What sort of names are those?"

"Old ones," said Stewart as he shook hands with his neighbor. The smile the two exchanged made it clear that Stewart hadn't been put off track at all by the aliases.

"I am Atana Potinija, but you can call me Minerva - or Athena," said the radiant blonde. Her hand felt comfortably warm to the touch and Stewart delighted in shaking it.

The beautiful one lunged outside, looked back once, and shuddered. "Rats! We've got rats, Medusa! Would you go in and shake your snakes at them - please?"

"Medusa?" said Erian with blatant disbelief.

Even Aiken looked up.

"Yeah, Medusa." Medusa glared at Erian a moment. "Coming." Her nimble fingers were untying her bandanna's knot already as she strode into the house.

With his arm braced over his eyes, 'Ares' ducked out of the house. "Hold it! Let me get out first before you turn me into a lawn ornament."

Athena propped her hand on her hip. "Actually, we could use some classical statuary to give this joint some class."

He uncovered his face and squared off with her. "I agree. Why don't you go inside?"

Athena smiled. "Age before beauty, big brother."

Aiken and Erian had been gawking all the while at the beautiful one, who had fixed her lustrous gaze upon them as she sashayed over to the fence.

Fairly drooling, Aiken leaned upon the fence. "If I didn't know any better, I'd say the Goddess of Love herself is standing here before me."

"How did you guess?" She batted her eyelashes at him. "And you must be Aiken."

Aiken's pleased smile faltered. "Hold on. How did you know my name?"

"Stewart told me," she replied.

Aiken fired a look at Stewart, but Stewart shook his head vehemently.

The instant Stewart glanced at Apollo and Athena though they grinned and shrugged. Something told him that they were panicking, just a little.

Aiken's unease floated away. "Seriously though, what is your name? I will be disappointed if it isn't Venus."

She smiled and smacked his hand with a lovely tap. "Then Venus it is! I'd hate to disappoint you."

Aiken smiled, but hesitated again. "Lovely, but, really, what IS your name?"

She smiled for an answer and shifted aside as the tall, alpha male of the bunch lunged forward.

"The name is Marshall," he said with a business-like tone that was as blunt as a hammer. "Is there something I can do for you?"

Shaking his head, Aiken backed off several steps, but his gaze remained fixed on the beautiful one.

Erian was just as suspicious as Stewart had been. "Let me see if I have this straight: Pajawone or Phoebus, Athena or Minerva, Marshall, Medusa, and Venus."

"You forgot Herman," said Athena.

"There's another one?" said Erian. In response to the stern stare Athena fixed upon him, he backed off toward their own back door. "Just clarifying things." Then as he ducked inside, he grumbled, "Bunch of nutters."

Aiken remained rooted to the spot grinning at Venus.

Typically, she smiled and simpered right back.

Wearing a stormy and over made up face, Udela popped open the back door and with a voice like a lightning's crack shouted, "Aiken!"

Aiken jumped. "What?"

"Phone!"

Aiken stomped inside. "Phone? You startle me over a phone call?" He sighed back at Venus. "I'll see you later."

"Of that I have no doubt whatsoever," said Venus.

Aiken paused at his back door to drink in that vision of loveliness smiling at him from beyond his fence.

However, as soon as the back door shut behind Aiken, shutting him inside with his mother's disapproval,

Venus dropped the pose with a roll of her eyes.

The chuckle that escaped from Stewart earned him several approving looks.

Bemused, Athena shook her head at Venus. "Shameless hussy."

Apollo joined in. "Just can't help yourself, can you, Aphrodite?"

"And how is your love life doing these days, Apollo dear?" Venus shot back.

Apollo's teasing grin did the Titanic and sank. "Rub it in, why don't you?" Even the sunlight seemed to dim ever so slightly.

Venus remained buoyant though as her sparkling eyes traveled from Apollo's dour face to Athena's disapproving one. "I've told you before, old man. If you need help, all you have to do is to invoke my assistance."

Apollo narrowed his eyes and cocked his head to the side. "Uh-huh."

"Seriously, Apollo dear."

"Oh. I am considering your offer – very carefully." He exchanged looks of mild alarm with Athena.

"All you have to do is ask." Venus narrowed her eyes at Athena and Apollo.

This was all a bit much. Stewart eyed all four strangers who gazed back with clear-eyed, open expressions. He backed away. "I have to go to – work. Yes, work. I'm going to be late."

Medusa stomped out of the derelict house. With a fierce tug, she secured the knot in her bandanna that kept her restless locks confined.

"Enjoy your snack?" said Mars.

"Oh ha ha ha. I bet you'll make a magnificent fountain ornament, Ares."

"It's Marshall. Marshall! Remember?"

Apollo cast a swift glance at Stewart, saw that he had heard their exchange, and grimaced.

Medusa rolled her eyes. "What? Having another identity crisis, are we?"

Venus laid a calming hand upon his arm. "Leave him be. People change their names all the time."

Marshall nodded. "That's right."

"Usually when they're wanted by the authorities," retorted Medusa.

Marshall and Medusa mouthed threats at each other, glaring red-eyed at one another the whole time. Apollo and Athena stepped out from between them – just in case.

Venus squeezed her lover's arm and smiled at Medusa. "So, what do you think of our pet project, Medusa?"

That stopped the snarling standoff.

Medusa glanced toward Stewart. "I like him."

Stewart felt stricken, deeply alarmed, almost electric.

Venus flexed her fingers and checked her nails. "I can't wait to get my hooks into that lump-of-manhood Aiken."

Stewart dashed inside and hiding just within, listened in.

Apollo let go a huge sigh and shook his head. "So much for discretion. I thought we were going to try to do this incognito?" His associates ignored his plaintive inquiry.

"You and Mars should team up on him," said Athena.

Mars shook his head. "Uhh. No, I've got a house to renovate, right, Apollo?"

"What?" said wide-eyed Apollo.

"Oh well, I'll just have to submarine his manly

confidence on my own," said Venus.

"Have fun, darling," said Mars.

Apollo jogged Athena in the arm. "You and I should work on Erian the brain."

"Who do I get to torment?" said Medusa.

Apollo draped his arm about her shoulders. "You, most excellent creature, are our secret weapon. We will unleash you only when the time is ripe."

"So don't go slithering off into any holes, love," said Mars.

Medusa glared at him and both resumed mouthing threats and gesticulating at one another until Athena cleared her throat.

The back door slammed again.

Stewart ducked back outside. His mother Udela was in a right foul mood now. Seeing her precious Aiken fall under the spell of the luscious hussy next door had her in the snit of all snits. His face wore an interesting mixture of misery and panic as he tugged on his overcoat and turned toward the gate.

"Rough morning, Stewart?" called Apollo.

"Aren't they all?" replied Stewart with a weak smile.

"My condolences," said Apollo.

Stewart nodded and trudged toward the gate.

Athena shook her head and spoke lowly, " 'Poor thing hasn't had a good day since that day his father passed."

Venus lunged toward the dividing fence and leaned upon it. "Watch!"

As tentative as a mouse, a young woman about Stewart's age had stopped at the Dunks' gate. For a moment, it looked as though she would keep walking as fast as her legs would carry her, but she stopped and lingered there watching him.

Stewart reached for the gate and as he did, looked up into her face. "Juliet!"

"Hello, Stewart." Juliet blushed and pressed her hands to her cheeks.

Their awkward silence gave way to smiles, but Stewart regained something of his normal, dour demeanor first. "Visiting?"

"'Moved back in with my Mum."

"And Roddy?"

"Divorced and good riddance too."

"Ah." Stewart's face brightened.

"I'm staying just for a little while, until I've figured out what I really want." Juliet smiled up at him. "Look at you. You look so professional."

Stewart's face went all pink and smiling. Juliet liked that look on him. She reached over the gate and brushed at his clothing.

"Work. I was just leaving."

Juliet stepped aside to let him come out. "I should let you go then."

Meanwhile, Venus crossed her fingers and muttered, "Come on. Come on."

Stewart took four shuffling steps down the sidewalk and stopped. For a moment he stood in a quagmire of indecision.

Still, Venus kept her fingers crossed. "Come on, son. It has been forever since you saw her."

Stewart looked back and Juliet's expression lit up, but he also saw his mother's bedroom curtain rise and the shadow of his mother's scowling face. That did it. "Meet me at five on the steps in front of the British Museum."

"The British Museum at Five then." Still wearing a smile as full as a sail in a stiff breeze, Juliet turned and marched down the sidewalk.

Stewart frowned at his house as he turned and set off at a hasty pace before something else unpleasant happened.

Venus did a little victory dance. "I knew he couldn't pass her up. I knew it."

Apollo nodded to himself. "He's ready for change."

Mars had his eyes on the Dunk household. "Now to create the space for him to wriggle free. Whoops! Look out."

The back door slammed. Udela was back. Hands set on her very round hips, she glared at her new neighbors.

"I'd sooner face my own mother than this battle ax." Mars grinned back with all the boyish charm he could muster.

"Look at it this way," muttered Medusa. "If she does thrash you, Hera WILL kick her ass for you."

"Are you calling me a Momma's boy?"

Medusa smiled ever so sweetly. "If the shoe fits…"

"Stifle it, you two," said Apollo. Then he spoke up. "Good morning, Mrs. Dunk."

Udela had a stare that even Medusa could appreciate, which she aimed at Apollo – for just one withering moment. Then she veered toward her gate and peered one way and then the other. The face she turned again toward her new neighbors reminded them of Cerberus when he had that bout of rabies a few years back, but they held their ground. After all, there stood a firm fence between them and this fearsome matriarch.

Apollo glanced at the broken gate though. Perhaps they should blockade it just in case.

Venus shifted between Mars and Apollo with one eye fixed on their own back door.

Apollo tried again. "'Quite a beautiful morning, don't you agree?"

Her voice emerged as a growl. "Erian said there were hippies next door."

"Hippies?" Apollo exchanged puzzled and vaguely piqued looks with the rest.

"I know your sort: naked orgiastic rituals every full moon, illegal substances, chanting at all hours…" Udela shook her formidable finger at them, but something about her tone suggested that she wouldn't be adverse to indulging in such behaviour given the opportunity.

"Hippies?" said Apollo again.

"I'm keeping my eye on you lot." Her gaze lingered on Mars and took on a different expression.

Mars shifted Venus in front of him.

Stunned, dumbfounded, amused, bemused, annoyed, pitying, and gawking, all five stared back over the fence at Udela. Even Hermes, who had been zipping past on the sidewalk, stopped to observe the confrontation. When Udela glanced his way though, Hermes ducked behind the fence before she could aim her sharp, fire engine red finger at him too.

Venus' chin tilted up and her brow cocked. She opened her mouth.

Udela wagged her finger in Venus' face. Apparently, she knew a minx, a real vixen, when she saw one. "And you – keep your filthy claws off my sons."

Venus frowned and checked her fingernails. "Oh! Thank you for reminding me. I really should get my nails done again." With that she turned away, utterly engrossed by her blunted manicure.

Udela gave them all a severe look, and turned back toward her house. She made certain to take Stewart's cup and plate with her and to set the lawn chair back precisely where it belonged. She paused though at her back door to glare towards the sidewalk. "You! Lurking behind the fence – that goes for you too."

Letting go a yelp, Hermes ran away.

In she went, but as soon as the door closed behind her however…

Apollo exploded with dismay. "HIPPIES?!"

"I told you that you needed a haircut, Apollo," said Mars.

"I had one two weeks ago."

Hermes returned. "Found the luggage!" All of which he began tossing over the fence.

As she stooped down to collect one of her own, Medusa ducked one of Venus' bags. "Where was it?"

"Albuquerque."

Athena ducked another piece of luggage. "Albuquerque! How in blazes did it end up there?"

"Turbulence."

"I warned you to lay off the beans, Hermes." Mars collected Venus' luggage about his feet.

Hermes stopped lobbing baggage. "Oh. Ha. Ha. Funny. It wasn't my fault. First, Pegasus hit a cold front over the Grand Canyon. Then some gun nut took a potshot at him. He did a power dive and our luggage ended up spread out all the way from Flagstaff to Albuquerque."

Venus picked up her beauty bag. "Better late than never. Let's unpack. Would you bring the rest in, sweetie?"

"Certainly, Pookie."

"That's my big cuddle bear." Venus caressed Mars' chin as she preceded him inside.

The others made faces.

Athena shuddered. "Ugh. I hate it when they baby

talk."

Medusa pushed past them with her luggage, grinning. "And your rooms are on either side of theirs. You're going to need earplugs."

Apollo faltered as Athena followed Medusa inside. "Hermes?"

Hermes trotted in past him, his stout sports bag in his arms. "Four sets of earplugs," said Hermes, "as soon as I've unpacked."

3. Friday Afternoon

Finally that week, Stewart passed an uneventful day. It was so quiet that it was a little dull or would have been but for the anticipation that made the day drag just a little bit.

Juliet. Juliet. Juliet. Juliet! Juliet was back and she was single again.

How he found the concentration to work he didn't know, but he filled the hours with careful industry laboring over the coin hoard. The day did pass, but nowhere near as quickly as he liked. All day long he practiced what he would say. He had come so far since they had been together last – that fateful night. He had a great job, just as she had used to wish for him to have, and he couldn't wait to tell her all about it.

In the back of his mind though, he wondered why she had run off with Roddy…when she had planned to run off with HIM. He tried to think of how he could broach the subject, but couldn't think of a way that wouldn't come out all wrong. He sighed and sat utterly still for a moment.

No, he couldn't press the issue. He was too happy that she was back and that she had sought him out. Smiling, Stewart resumed his work and wished for 5 pm to arrive.

One thing was certain, Stewart was having a better day than his new neighbors were.

Looking something akin to a toxic tropical flower in hopes of catching the eye of that tall athletic brute next door, Udela puttered about her garden and hummed to herself. Normally, the only things that would have disrupted her chores would have been one of her other neighbors poking her head over the fence to gossip or a particularly special 'visitor'. The new neighbors were an industrious lot, which quite surprised Udela. All day her stubborn concentration had been shattered time and again by the sounds of random destruction emanating from the house next door. Yells, shouts, yelps, yowls, thuds, thunks, bangs, crashes, and now and then a sound she could not quite define resounded courtesy of those strange people.

At the far end of the yard, from which arose the aroma of freshly clipped grass, stood a cloth-covered, red picnic table with green benches. Alongside the house, pails of paint stood in a soldierly line. Each one was labeled: dining room, bedroom 1, bedroom 2, and so forth.

"Look out! Look out!" shouted Marshall.

Bang! The whole house next door shook and then reverberated.

Udela jumped and pressed her hand to her bosom.

"Hot-dammit!" the same loud voice roared. "Hermes!"

The scruffy young man wearing a baseball cap emblazoned with a golden wing logo hurtled through the door and out the gate as though Old Beelzebub himself were right on his heels.

And indeed, the large footballer swooped out directly after him.

Udela watched the brawny man chase the lean one up and down and up and down the sidewalk. Finally, she heard a yelp from halfway down the lane.

The big man returned, dragging the smaller one by his right ear.

"Ow. Ow. Ow. Ow."

"Shut up, you big baby."

The back screen door opened and banged shut. The tall fire-haired man and the serene, sharp-eyed blonde supported the African lady outside between them. They laid her out on the picnic table and, patting her hands and cheeks, shook her gently.

"Come back to us, old priestess," said Apollo as he paused to peek under her eyelids.

Medusa opened her eyes, cried out, and then covered eyes with her arm. "You've got two heads!"

Stepping nimbly aside, the luscious brunette ventured outside just as Mars shoved Hermes inside ahead of him. She paused to smile prettily in Udela's direction, causing Udela to attack her roses.

"Now clean up that mess." Mars shoved Hermes toward the back door.

Hermes balked in the doorway. "Make me!"

"Fix that mess OR I tell Medusa who dropped the refrigerator on her."

Hermes cast a look of stark terror toward Medusa. "I'm going. I'm going." He ducked inside.

Apollo finished examining Medusa's head. "Could someone get some ice? Medusa, darling, you're going to have a lovely little mountain peak atop your cranium."

"I'll get the ice." Venus went back in.

Apollo called after her. "And some aspirin too, if you would please."

Venus shouted back out, "Whatever you say, Doc."

Mars lingered beside the back door, but then he

made the mistake of meeting Udela Dunk's stare from across the fence.

Udela addressed him in very arch tones. "Do you plan to continue making an almighty racket all day?"

Mars smiled with sudden boyish charm. He risked a few steps in her direction. "Only all weekend." He rather enjoyed the little wince that crossed her face. "A little racket is unavoidable when renovations are underway."

Udela was as quick as ever to sniff out an opportunity. Her tone changed. "So you do home repairs, do you?"

Mars' smile froze in place. He knew precisely what that tone implied and he could just imagine the sort of household 'honey do' list a woman like Udela could come up with. "We are renovating this house – JUST this house."

"And do you plan to live in it afterwards?"

"Uh, no."

"Ah. I see." She batted her eyelashes. She actually batted her false eyelashes at him.

Mars took on a crooked grin. She had no idea the sort of wickedness his own twisted mind was capable of, but he had just decided that he would be more than willing for her to find out.

"So you do work for hire as a handyman of sorts?"

"I could, but we're on a tight schedule to fix the problems here before we move on to our next assignment," said Mars. He met Apollo's suspicious glance and gave a short shrug.

With a book - 'Household Wiring for Cretans' – in hand, Hermes sauntered out, whistling.

Mars lunged at him. "Done already?"

"Yes, Master," yawned Hermes.

"The WHOLE mess?"

"Yes, Master."

Venus returned with a little plastic bag full of ice, a plastic cup full of water, and a pair of aspirins. Medusa propped herself up with a groan as Athena applied the ice to Medusa's head and Apollo administered the aspirin.

Meek, for once, Medusa accepted their ministrations, but finally, she eased off the picnic table, tested her balance a moment, and then stood on her own. "I'm going to lie down and wait for the aspirin to kick in."

"Very well," said Apollo. "Let us know if you need anything."

Medusa shuffled inside with the ice pressed hard to her head. "Yeah. Yeah." She muttered. She stopped though and jabbed a sharp fingernail toward Hermes, who quailed behind his open book. "I'll fix you later."

Hermes darted just past Apollo and Athena, so that they and the picnic table stood between him and Medusa's spark throwing glance, just in case he needed to duck in a big hurry.

Medusa's upper lip curled at him, but then she winced, and shuffled inside.

All the while Udela fairly tapped her toes with impatience. There were pipes to be replaced, shelves to be built, walls that needed a fresh coat of paint. Oh so much to be done. "Are you sure that I can't lure you over for some extra chores? I am willing to pay, if your fee is reasonable," she said.

Mars exchanged a look of half-strangulated alarm with Apollo. She would be the sort to hover over one too all the while there was work to be done, fussing over how one held the wrench, drooling with compliments at how one turned a screw. He began to have second thoughts, a rare occurrence for him.

"Oh, I'm certain the lads here could negotiate some sort of fee in exchange for their labors," said Venus as she smiled from Mars to Apollo.

Apollo's gaze sharpened. "Leave me out of this." He yanked the book out of Hermes' hands and buried his nose deep in its pages.

Taking care to smile over at Udela, Venus took Mars aside. "Do this for poor Stewart and Juliet. I'm sure you'll find a way to have a little fun with it all."

"You can't possibly mean that," he said.

She pinched him and shoved him toward the fence. "This isn't about us. Now get over there."

Mars took on a sober, business-like demeanor. "Well, Mrs. Dunk, you wore me down. Write up a list and WE…" Mars looked at both Apollo and Hermes, who cringed. "…will come over later so you can give us an official tour of all the problem sites."

"I will have the list shortly." Almost giddy at the prospect, Udela flew through her back door into her house, but as soon as her back door closed…

"We?" said Apollo. "What is this WE stuff?"

"I'm not dealing with that overheated basilisk alone," said Mars in a tone that brooked no refusal. "You aren't wriggling out of this one." Mars pointed his finger at Apollo and then at Hermes. "And don't get any smart ideas about dropping a piano on your foot either. Got that? Right then." Mars stomped inside.

"He didn't mention safes." Hermes perked up. "I could drop a safe on you, Apollo."

Mars' voice came out through the back door. "No, he couldn't!"

"Long-eared jackass," groused Hermes.

"I heard that!"

Hermes made a face toward the back door.

Athena grinned in spite of herself. "Stop while you're ahead, Hermes. You're in enough trouble for one day."

Venus sidled up beside Hermes and draped her arm across his shoulders. His impish face flushed pink. He fairly fidgeted with delight.

"I know just the thing to keep our wing-footed youth out of trouble. We need groceries. Take this list." She tucked a neatly folded paper into the palm of his hand.

Hermes gave her a dirty look as he unfolded the list and studied it. A look of consternation rose upon his face. "What the hell - ?"

"I want everything on this list. Can you do that and be back in an hour?"

"But these mushrooms - they're scattered all over the world," said Hermes.

"Umhmm. I'm cooking a special mushroom stew for dinner tonight."

With a pat on his shoulders and a peck for his cheek, which he scarcely noticed, Venus sashayed back inside, serenely oblivious to the looks of burgeoning dread and outright horror spreading across the faces of Hermes, Apollo, and Athena.

Hermes seized Apollo's sleeve. "I heard her say it. She said 'cook'."

"Worse," said Athena, "she said 'cooking' – present tense."

Apollo winced and pried Hermes' hands loose. "Which means she's already started."

Athena stood stock still. "It's going to be Valhalla all over again."

Hermes seized a hold of Apollo's arm again. "Flames everywhere."

Apollo struggled free of Hermes at last and pushed him toward the gaping gate. "You'd better go. If you aren't back in an hour, we'll never hear the end of it."

Hermes turned his cap backwards and pocketed the list as he trudged toward the sidewalk. "Maybe I'll get sucked up by a tornado on the way back."

Athena thought it best to take her mind away from the inevitable, so she peered over Apollo's shoulder at the book. "Do you think we could fix the wiring on our own?"

Apollo closed the paperback book with a resounding slap. "Of course we can! How hard can it be?"

Apollo headed inside. Athena followed. The book lay abandoned upon the picnic table, ominously pristine, still possessed of its new book aroma.

Mars bumped and stomped outside with more debris for the rubbish heap, whistling Sousa all the way. He dumped the rubbish over the fence onto the heap.

A strange buzzing sound flooded out of the house. Frowning, he turned as, briefly, once, twice, and then finally, for an excruciatingly prolonged spell, every light in the house came on, accompanied by loud buzzing. Then all the lights went out.

In the darkened silence within, Medusa's voice rang out, "What the Hell was that?"

Not waiting to find out, she and Venus dashed outside. They stopped beside Mars and eyed the house.

After several prods from Venus, Mars ventured back inside as though he expected to find a monster waiting.

The back door had scarcely swung shut when it

swung open again and out marched Apollo and Athena. Their blackened right hands smoldered. Both wore expressions of puzzlement as they sat upon the picnic table bench and eyed their smoking fingertips.

"You know, it's a good thing we're Gods," said Apollo, "or it might have actually…"

Athena sniffed at her fingers and wrinkled her nose. " …Hurt."

Apollo picked up the book with his left hand and, balancing it on his knees, opened it, flipping through several pages. He stopped abruptly and studied a page. "Ohhh! We forgot to ground the wires!"

"Oh, so that's it!" Athena rolled her eyes and flexed her fingers with a little effort.

Venus approached them. "What happened?"

"Just a little unscheduled electric shock therapy," said Apollo.

Athena smirked. "I'm feeling so much better now."

Venus gave Athena a smug smile and began to walk past. "Well. Well. It looks like we can't do everything after all, Miss Know-it-all."

Athena reached out with her right hand and thumped her.

ZAP! POP!

"Ow!" Venus scrambled off to the other side of Apollo, rubbing her well rounded behind.

"Hmmmm." Athena eyed her blackened index finger.

Apollo stood up and faced Venus. "Pardon me a moment, dear, but I need to see something." With that he touched her on the shoulder, ever so lightly, ever so fleetingly with his own blackened index finger.

ZAP-POW!

"Ow!" Venus ran all the way past Medusa and glared at Apollo.

Apollo turned his keen grin toward Athena. "You know what this means, don't you?"

Both exchanged sudden and very wicked grins.

"Let's zap Ares," said Athena.

Chortling fiendishly, Athena and Apollo charged inside.

Athena's voice drifted outside. "Oh, Ares, brother dear, could we see you for a moment?"

Medusa and Venus braced themselves.

"Marshall. It's MAR-SHALL!"

The silence was brief, but seemed to last a small, cringing eternity. Then a bright light flashed through every window. It was accompanied by a thunderous pop. The yelp that accompanied it was to be expected.

So was the sight of Athena and Apollo tearing forth from the house and racing through the gaping gate onto and then down the sidewalk in opposite directions. The bristling figure of Mars blurring after them was no surprise whatsoever.

Fortunately, Medusa and Venus had the presence of mind to be standing close to the dividing fence and not between their back door and the gaping gate. From that position, they could enjoy nearly all of the action.

First, they saw Mars run one way with Apollo scampering just ahead of him. Then Mars ran back the other way, gaining on Athena this time.

Breathless, Mars returned, but wearing a fierce and triumphant grin. Trapped in the crook of his brawny arm, he dragged Athena along beside him back into the yard and toward the back door. "Let's play a game. It's called: how long does it take to cram a goddess into a dishwasher?"

Apollo sauntered back, but only as far as the broken gate, the post of which he leaned upon.

His old, unsinkable jaunty self, Hermes trooped forth up the sidewalk, swinging two shopping bags. He handed the bags to Apollo, who glanced inside them, and then handed them on to Venus.

"Yours," said Apollo.

Hermes sized up the general mood. "I missed something. What did I miss?"

"Athena's getting a thrashing from Mars," said Medusa.

Hermes' face lit up. "Really? What did she do?"

Apollo held up his sore hand. "Electricity. It's a wondrous thing."

"How come he isn't thrashing you?" said Hermes.

"Because I could run faster."

The Dunks' back door opened. Out came Udela with several sheets of paper crammed with neat, tight purple handwriting. Hermes ducked and pressed himself against the fence.

"What's wrong with you?" said Apollo as he turned. He saw. He froze. "Oh."

Udela handed Apollo the papers. "There are just a few projects. Where is your friend?"

The look of gobsmacking horror that struck Apollo's face caused Medusa to cover her mouth before a giggle betrayed her.

"This is what you call a 'few' projects?" said Apollo.

Looking pleased, Mars stomped back outside. Thrashing Athena always put him in a good mood for hours afterward.

Apollo shoved the tidy, but substantial list into his hands.

Mars' jaw dropped.

Udela smiled at him. "These are merely the worst problems I've been having – the ones that absolutely require fixing. Just a few projects, as I told your friend here."

"Fine." Mars swallowed his panic. "Let's discuss terms."

"Thirty pounds an hour – each," said Apollo.

"Ten," said Udela, her smile turning sharp and hard.

"Thirty," said Apollo.

"Five."

"FIVE?" cried Apollo.

Udela smiled and batted those fake eyelashes at Mars.

Mars laid a hand briefly on Apollo's shoulder and said, "How about this? Whatever materials we buy, you pay for, Mrs. Dunk. Deal?"

"Deal! I will expect you at ten sharp tomorrow morning. I'll give you the tour."

"We'll be there," said Mars as he glanced through the whole length and breadth of the list.

His companions marveled at how steadily Mars beamed charm and good humor in Udela's direction. He even returned her little wave. The instant she had closed her back door behind her though...

"A FEW projects?" said Mars. "It's more like a whole new house she wants."

Hermes poked his head back up. "She's gone. Finally!"

"You do realize of course that she has no intention of reimbursing us for anything," said Apollo.

The gleam in Mars' eyes brightened and his smile both widened and sharpened. He laughed lowly. It was a deliciously ominous sound. "She's going to be sorry she hired us. Medusa?"

"Yes, Mar-shall?"

"Cute."

Medusa batted her eyelashes.

"How would you like to take up interior decoration?" said Mars.

"Do I get to pick the colors and so forth?"

"You can pick whatever your little serpentine heart desires, darling."

"I'm in!"

"In the meantime, we'd best finish what we started in our own little hovel." Mars sighed and led the march back in.

4. Friday Evening: Five And Sevenish PM

Halfway afraid that she wouldn't be there, Stewart delayed his departure for five minutes. Then suddenly afraid that Juliet might leave, he rushed out to find her. He spied her at once, but did not hurry to join her on the steps. For a long moment he savored the sight of her looking about through the throngs for him. She consulted her wristwatch and shifted his way with a searching gaze.

Immediately he was sorry that he had made her wait. Anxiety lined her face, but then she locked eyes with Stewart. Her face lit up an instant before she smiled. It was as though they had never been apart.

Hand in hand, Stewart and Juliet set off.

It was just shy of seven.

Aiken had quit work much earlier just so he could stand at the fence and leer at his new neighbor Venus as she set out the bread plates and soup bowls on the picnic table. Incorrigible as always, Venus liked attention. Her every motion as she set the table was done in the most beguiling manner possible.

Medusa came outside, rolled her eyes at the spectacle, and set two baskets of plain sliced bread on the table. As Venus turned about to arrange them in the center, Medusa stepped between her backside and Aiken, folded her arms across her breast and glared.

Aiken walked away from the fence and pretended

to be watching for someone on the sidewalk.

Medusa rounded on Venus. "Shameless hussy."

"Oh! Was that the pot calling the kettle black? That's bold talk for someone who was caught fornicating in Athena's temple."

"At least I didn't start a war over a golden apple, and besides, as you will recall, I paid a pretty severe price for my transgression." Medusa tugged at one of her sinuous braids and then dragged a finger across her neck.

Athena stomped outside bearing pitchers brimming with sparkling refreshment in each hand. Her stride faltered though at the sharp looks Venus and Medusa threw at her. "What?"

Stone cold silence.

Athena set the pitchers on the table and wiped off her hands. "Whatever it is, I didn't do it."

If she had had a tail, it would have wagged. Venus lived for these opportunities to mix it up. "Actually, you DID, right, Medusa?"

"She certainly did," said Medusa.

Athena rolled her eyes. "You can't be sore about that still?"

"You turned me into a monster," spat Medusa.

"You were fornicating in my temple."

"You over-reacted," said Medusa.

"Which is what she always does," added Venus.

"All we were doing was…"

"Fucking in my temple!" Athena shouted, "There is NO FUCKING IN MY TEMPLE! Look, next time, go to Dionysus' temple. He likes to watch."

"And how would you know that?" said Medusa.

"Everyone knows that," said both Athena and Venus.

Then Venus leaned toward Medusa. "Say the

word and I'll take care of Athena for you."

"Don't you dare," cried Athena. "If I catch so much as a whiff of that trigger happy delinquent you call a son, Aphrodite, I'll turn him into a worm and Psyche into the early bird. Got it?"

"Yeah, Venus, you wouldn't want that to happen now, would you?" said Medusa.

"Look! I've apologized for that." Suddenly Athena understood how a bull felt in the presence of a matador even as she watched Venus sidle up to her.

"Why did you have Perseus…"

"That psychopath!" corrected Medusa.

"…cut off Medusa's head?"

Athena sighed and flung her hands up from her sides. "It had power and I needed to borrow it."

Medusa was on the verge of a right unholy conniption fit. "Borrow it?!"

Aiken risked a look at them. Luckily, they did not see his odd look or arched brow.

"Look!" said Athena. "I made amends. You not only got your head back, but your looks too."

"I still have snakes for hair," said Medusa.

"Those powers remain intact for a reason," said Athena, "and I know you've put them to good use. The Date Rape Avenger? 'Ring any bells?"

Medusa looked about.

Aiken looked away before she could see the acute look of unease on his face. That name had rung a bell for him somewhere.

Medusa lowered her voice, "No one was supposed to know about that."

"Medusa, there aren't many folks running about who can turn people to stone," said Venus. "It was a dead giveaway."

Medusa heaved a huge sigh, but still glared at her old nemesis.

Aiken shook his head. Except for that lovely bird who insisted that he call her Venus, they were a strange lot. He ventured a little closer again now that they seemed to be chatting as opposed to snarling at one another. "How are our lovely Graces today?"

Medusa frowned. "I think they're on holiday still. Was it Bali or Pango Pango?"

Venus batted her eyelashes at Aiken. "We're fine. You and your flattery, Aiken."

Medusa rolled her eyes. "I'll go get the napkins."

Equally repulsed by their flirting, Athena turned to follow her. "I'll get the glasses."

"Stir the stew while you're in there, and don't let Herman or Marshall slip any more wine into it," said Venus.

As soon as the door closed behind them, Aiken said, "Alone at last."

Venus leaned upon the fence. "How was your day, Mr. Dunk?"

"Lonely. And yours?"

"Mine wasn't the least bit lonely but then I know how to occupy myself." Venus stuck her tongue out.

A crash resounded from the renovated house behind her. Venus' flirty, simpering smile didn't falter in the least.

"Damn it, Hermes," bellowed Mars.

"What in bloody hell are you lot doing over there?" said Aiken.

"Renovations," said Venus with a shrug.

"It sounds like you're tearing the house down."

Another horrific crash shook the house.

Mars' voice roared forth. "Look. If you're trying

to kill me, just do it."

Medusa chimed in. "Do it, Hermes. Do it."

"Don't start with me, Medusa," said Mars. "Not today."

Venus tapped Aiken's hand to draw his attention back. "Actually, Marshall and Phoebus are supposed to start working on your house tomorrow."

Aiken didn't look happy to hear that. "What?"

"First thing in the morning." She smiled. "It was your Mother's idea. She's really looking forward to it."

"I think I need to have a chat with her."

"You do that."

Aiken headed for his back door, grumbling, "Not another of her boyfriends."

Another bang accompanied the sound of plates crashing. Even Venus had to turn and wonder at that. Aiken stopped, his hand on the doorknob.

Donning his jacket, Mars stomped outside. He gave her a sheepish look and a shrug as he headed out onto the sidewalk. "We need plates."

Venus met Aiken's alarmed glance before he ducked into his home.

Hermes stuck his head outside. "Is he gone?"

"Is who gone?" she said.

"Ares."

"He went to buy some plates."

"Ha!" Bearing a brimming pitcher, Hermes came outside grinning. He sat on the end of the picnic table facing her and let his feet swing. "It wasn't my fault this time. Mars broke all of the dishes."

"He didn't knock my stew off the stove, did he?"

"No – unfortunately."

"What?"

"Nothing."

"You lot have no confidence in me. It's shameful really," said Venus.

"All that matters is that you have confidence in yourself." Hermes winked and gave her the thumbs up.

Uncertain whether he was being sincere or sarcastic Venus stared at him.

Hermes grinned harmlessly. He was trying for innocent, but there were limits even to his acting skills. His glance traveled past Venus toward the fence. Suddenly, he clasped his hands together and struck a pose. "Romeo. Oh Romeo. Wherefore art thou, Romeo?"

"What?" said Venus.

Hermes jerked his thumb toward the fence. "Lover-boy's back. Why don't you ask him how his date went?"

Venus looked. Indeed, Stewart was creeping past their shattered, battered abode toward his own overly bright homestead. His gaze was fixed upon its windows and doors, behind which stillness seemed to malinger.

Venus hailed him. "Stewart! How did…?"

"What I do is my own concern, Aiken," Udela snapped over her shoulder as she charged out from around the front. "And you! Sneaking in from the back. Where have you been?"

"Out with a friend," said Stewart.

"And you couldn't find a minute to ring me so that I wouldn't keep dinner waiting?"

"Since when have you ever held anything for me?" said Stewart. "Besides, Erian does all the cooking anymore. If I should apologize to anyone, it should be him."

Their ears primed to catch every syllable, Venus and Hermes exchanged looks.

Udela bristled not only because he was right, but because he had the temerity to say as much.

Despite his bluster, Stewart edged past his mother as he would a rabid dog on the end of a chain. "I wasn't hungry anyway."

"You ate already, I see."

"Just chips and such."

Venus was at Stewart's side in a blink and had her hands linked about his right arm. She fixed her dazzling smile upon Udela. "Then perhaps he can have stew with us tonight? I need an objective verdict. My friends don't think I can cook."

"You'd be better off with your brother's cold leftovers," said Hermes in all sincerity.

"See what I mean?" The severe, scalding look Venus fixed on Hermes caused him to duck back inside like a whipped dog. "Let him picnic with us, Mrs. Dunk, that way you can have the rest of the night to do as you please. You have another date tonight perhaps?"

For an instant, Udela gave her a puzzled look. It hadn't occurred to her how obvious her conduct was, but she remained immune to Venus' charm, and yet, being able to relax the rest of the evening appealed mightily to her selfishness, which Venus was counting on. Still, she stood immovable and with over-painted eyes eyed the beautiful one.

"If you're afraid I might corrupt him somehow, just send Aiken or Erian over to mind him."

Stewart gave Venus a look suggesting that she had lost her reason. She gave him a look that said, 'Trust me'. Then she squeezed his arm and pressed close to his side as though she were his big sister.

Finally, Udela took on a tight, hard little smile. "A little peace and quiet tonight just might do the trick."

With that she sailed back into her home.

Two seconds later, she shoved Erian outside. One second after that, Aiken found himself shoved outside as well.

Stewart sighed and hung his head.

"Never fear," said Venus. "We have a plan."

"A plan? Why do I not like the sound of that?"

Mars trudged back through the gate. He held up two shopping bags.

"Perfect timing," said Venus. "Dinner should be ready now."

Mars' stride faltered. He fixed a grimace upon his face, hoping that it looked as though he possessed at least a smidgen of enthusiasm about the impending ordeal. In he went.

"Come on over, lads, and have dinner with us." Venus focused her charming smile on Aiken and Erian, drawing them after her to the picnic table, but she kept her arms wrapped about Stewart to keep him from fleeing. Bodily she steered him up to the table. "Have some stew and tell me what you think, Stewart. It's a special recipe."

As Aiken and Erian entered the yard, Hermes crossed their path to sit on the rain barrel at the far end of the picnic table. "Run while you still can," he muttered. He set a stack of paper cups on the table, taking one for himself.

Venus' glance was sharp and swift. "What was that?"

"Nothing." Hermes hid his face in his hands. If he had been wearing a cowl, he would have resembled a monk lost in desperate prayer.

Venus sat the Dunk boys toward the opposite end so that Hermes wouldn't upset them with his teeth gnashing. "Dinner will be served shortly."

In she went.

From the pitcher, Hermes sloshed what looked like punch into his cup. He held it up with the expression of a man hearing his fatal sentence pronounced and said, "Prosit!" Down went the cup's entire contents. He winced with painful pleasure and gave a sharp little coyote yip. "Want some?"

"What is it?" said Aiken.

"Ruby red grapefruit juice, citrus punch, pomegranate juice, and Vodka. Yum. Yum." Hermes had picked up the pitcher already and was refilling his cup.

There was a mad scramble after cups and Hermes filled each to its brim. Then he held up his cup again. "To a merry and wayward life."

"Cheers," said Aiken.

They downed their drinks. Hermes smacked his lips and made other sounds of satisfaction. The three Dunks winced, gasped, and made various inarticulate noises. Then they stared into their cups, dazed.

"More?" said Hermes.

All three held out their cups. Wearing a cunning smile, Hermes refilled them.

"Shouldn't that pitcher be getting emptier?" said Erian, the smart Dunk brother.

Hermes winked. "It should, but it won't." He held up his cup and looked right at Stewart. "Here's to second chances."

Stewart paused. There was no mistaking Hermes' meaning. He smiled to himself as he raised his cup. "To second chances."

"Second chances at what?" said Aiken.

"Everything," said Hermes. "Down the hatch!"

They downed their drinks again and succumbed to spasms from which they all emerged ruddy and smiling.

"There, now I'm ready," said Hermes.

"Ready for what?" said Erian.

Venus came outside bearing a large stew pot. "Dinner is ready. Where is everybody?"

Hermes grumbled into his cup, "Hiding under the furniture most likely."

"Stewart, be a dear and take this for me," said Venus.

Stewart collected the stewpot from her and set it in the center of the table, while Venus went back inside with her sleeves rolled up.

"It smells good," Aiken called after her.

Hermes snorted.

Bemused, Stewart sat and smiled into his cup. Juliet. Juliet. Juliet. Yes, a second chance with Juliet and suddenly all things seemed possible, as they never had before. Suddenly everything seemed bearable if she were in his life.

"So, what does this second chances bit mean, Stew?" said Aiken.

"You didn't know? Juliet is back," said Erian. "She was out by the gate this morning. You remember her. She had our Stew wrapped around her little finger for years. Like two peas in a pod they were. Then one day she runs off with someone else without so much as a farewell note. Stew was in the dumps for the longest time. Remember?"

Aiken smiled, and an ugly one it was too. "Yeah, I remember her. I have fond memories of her."

"You teased her enough," grumbled Stewart.

Aiken's smile grew even nastier, if that could be possible.

Erian observed the dark looks that passed between his brothers. "Didn't you ask her out once?" he said.

Stewart's gaze hardened upon Aiken's smiling face.

"As a matter of fact, I did," said Aiken.

"And?" said Stewart.

Aiken smiled and seemed about to reply when Medusa, Athena, Apollo, and Mars stumbled out the back door. Hard behind them came Venus as stern and relentless as a cowboy riding herd.

Medusa and Athena set out the extra bowls, the glasses, and spoons they had brought. Apollo set out a long cloth-covered breadbasket from which the aroma of freshly toasted garlic swirled. Mars dumped a stack of napkins in the middle of the table and sat at the head of the table, opposite of Hermes in his boozy sulk. Mars' demeanor suggested a man facing execution via indigestion of the most exotic nature: he was bracing himself for the inevitable bellyache to end all bellyaches.

Medusa, Athena, and Apollo sat upon the bench as well and clung instinctively to one another as Venus took up the industrial-sized ladle and gave each a serving that nearly overflowed from their bowls.

"What are we having again?" said Athena.

"Mushroom stew from a very special recipe," said Venus.

At last all of the bowls stood full, to the brim, with a steaming, brownish mixture chock full of mushrooms. Nobody touched their spoons, not even the Dunks, who found themselves suddenly infected with inexplicable caution.

"You know I fussed over this stew. These are fresh spices in here. I ground them up or picked them myself. I sent Hermes all over the place to find just the right mushrooms."

"All over?" said Mars.

Hermes rubbed his face in his hands. "Japan, Germany, France, China, Africa, Italy, North America, Mexico, South America…"

Apollo snapped to attention. "Where in South America?"

"Peru."

"Peru!"

"You need a certain special Peruvian mushroom to give the recipe the right kick," said Venus.

"Where did you get this recipe? If you don't mind my asking," said Apollo.

"From the Oracle at Delphi."

"You got this from those hop-heads at Delphi?" cried Apollo.

"Yes, of course." Venus frowned at his reaction.

"Christ!" said Apollo.

Hermes cackled. "You'll be seeing him soon enough."

"Oh, God," said Medusa.

"Him too," said Hermes.

Stewart and Erian exchanged frowns and mouthed, 'Oracle at Delphi?'

"I'm beginning to be insulted. Will no one taste my stew?" Arms crossed over her breast, Venus' glare settled upon Mars.

Mars stirred his stew, delaying the inevitable. "Just savoring the aroma. Did you use wine?"

"Aside from the wine you sneaked in? No. I used ambrosia actually. The Oracle suggested it as an alternative."

Apollo grumbled to Athena, "Remind me to have a little chat with the Oracle later."

Athena grumbled back, "Certainly, but you're

assuming that I'll have a mind left with which to remind you of anything."

Beneath the intensifying browbeating, Mars churned his stew now, a smile of sorts frozen on his face beneath Venus' glare.

Mars raised his spoon. "Here goes nothing." Stew dripped from it. Steam wound sinuously upward, weaving like a drunken cobra. He took a very careful sip from his spoon, held it in his mouth for a moment, and then ate the entire spoonful.

Apollo, Athena, Medusa, and Hermes leaned toward him.

"His head hasn't started spinning," said Hermes.

" 'No smoke coming out of his ears," said Athena.

"His eyes aren't shooting flames," said Apollo.

"But how does it taste?" said Medusa.

Mars finished chewing on the mushrooms and dipped his spoon into the bowl. "Rather good actually. Tuck in."

Erian and Aiken plunged into their meal.

After a few test slurps, Apollo and the rest began to eat. Still standing, Venus nibbled on some garlic bread, which she dipped in her bowl.

Stewart sat stirring his stew though. "So, Aiken, what did Juliet say when you asked her out?"

Aiken took on that ugly grin Hermes had observed earlier. "She told me to bugger off."

For a long moment, Stewart and Aiken sat with their gazes locked.

"What did you do to her?" said Stewart.

"What makes you think I did anything?" said Aiken.

Medusa paused eating and reached for a slice of plain bread, but her entire attention was focused on their conversation.

"What did you do?" said Stewart.

"What does it matter?" said Erian between bites. "She dumped you ages ago."

Stewart sloshed his spoon around in his stew and then shoved it away. "I'm not hungry after all." He stood up. His angry gaze remained locked with Aiken's cold, amused one.

"Are you sure of that?" said Venus.

"I'm sorry."

"Very well. Some other time." She frowned at Aiken.

Off Stewart marched, straight through the gaping gate and down the sidewalk.

Although it wasn't his intention, his steps turned toward Juliet's former home. All the way there the look on Aiken's face spurred Stewart on. It had never occurred to him that something might have happened, something other than himself, to drive Juliet away. She had married Roddy and moved away at the same time, so he hadn't been able to talk to her. He remembered her own mother's embarrassed confusion and, in the end, sympathy, but she couldn't help him. Juliet wasn't talking then. The same question rolled over and over in his mind: 'What happened, Juliet?'

Her mother seemed surprised to see him, but she pulled him inside fast enough and propelled him into the kitchen where Juliet smiled over a pot of goulash she was stirring.

Juliet's father arrived from work soon after and greeted Stewart as though nothing had ever changed. For a moment, Stewart would have gladly embraced that illusion, but then he caught the looks her parents exchanged behind Juliet's back. Unsettling looks of concern mingled with relief. It struck him that they were as happy to have her back as he was.

What HAD happened to Juliet?

Then they turned and smiled at him.

"The goulash is ready," said Juliet, turning toward them. "Oh? Did I tell you? Stewart works at the British Museum. Just as he always intended to do."

Stewart's uneasy question remained unasked.

5. Saturday: Stewart's Morning

Waking up on Juliet's parents' sofa did not surprise Stewart. He remembered being offered the use of it by her parents who seemed even more eager than Juliet to keep him about, although Juliet kept finding excuses to delay his going home. They needn't have tried so hard.

Now that Juliet was back the last thing Stewart cared to do was go home to his desperately aging mother and two older brothers. Udela could be a right unholy haranguing terror if she didn't have a date to meet on the weekend or if things just didn't go her way. Frankly, she wasn't that much easier to endure if she did get what she wanted because she always wanted more. Invariably, she came home stinking of drink, a mess, a fright, and tangled up with some man who should have, or would have, known better if he wasn't equally pickled. Erian avoided the unpleasant squalor of it all by holing up in his room with his electronics while Stewart read with music blaring through his earphones. Aiken had made it a habit long ago to simply stay out until Monday night rolled around again.

Therefore, waking up on Juliet's parent's couch was a pleasure. Her parents' Chihuahua Nacho lay curled up beside Stewart's head, giving off little doggy grunts and snores.

Waking up to find Juliet nestled against him, snug in his embrace, was pure, serene bliss. He watched the pale curtains glow warm from the first rays of fresh sunlight as he breathed in the subtle perfume of aloe vera from Juliet's moisturizer. He dared not move for fear of waking her and destroying his idyll.

An idyll, yes, that's what it was, at last, an idyll.

Upstairs her parents shuffled and thumped about. Soon they would come down the creaking stairs. Juliet stirred and sighed, and stretching a little, groaned and burrowed back into sleep, pressing closer against him. For a long moment she lay as heavily as before, but she stirred again and rubbed her face.

"Good morning, Juliet," Stewart murmured.

She turned her face. She was smiling. "Morning, Stew. Hungry?"

Beaming, Stewart nodded. Juliet sat up. Nacho promptly moved into her abandoned space, curled up in her warm spot, sighed deeply and resumed napping.

On the landing above, a door opened. Footsteps trod dully on the stairs.

Juliet leaned down and kissed him lightly, happily, and slipped out. "Morning, Mum!"

"Morning. Is Stewart still here?" she said in a hushed voice.

"Yes. You don't have to whisper. He's awake." Juliet darted upstairs just past her mother, who peered in at Stewart and Nacho.

"Morning," Stewart said.

She smiled indulgently, the way his own mother could never be bothered to smile at him. "Hungry?"

"Yes, actually."

"Get up then and I'll fix breakfast."

Between Juliet and her mother, Stewart wound up well and truly stuffed.

Her father kept the coffee coming. "What have

you planned for today?"

"Nothing. Absolutely nothing," said Stewart.

"I have to go shopping," said Juliet. "We need milk, potatoes, and such. Why don't you come with me?"

"Gladly," said Stewart.

The pair had not gone far when they encountered the evidence of a chaotic night. It was as though the whole neighborhood were nursing a hangover and Stewart's new neighbors seemed to have played a role in it all, although he hesitated admitting that he knew who they were.

Someone had spray painted, 'The Date Rape Avenger Is Watching You' on the walls and sidewalks outside every pub and nightclub in the immediate vicinity. Everywhere they went Juliet and he saw proprietors either getting rid of the enigmatic warnings or puzzling over them.

People in his neighborhood were also full of amazed excitement about the latest outrageous thefts of public art from London: the statues of King Richard the Lionheart and of Boudicca and her daughters right along with their chariot and horses had disappeared from the vicinity of Westminster overnight. Witnesses claimed to have seen a possible perpetrator, but they also claimed to have seen the said perpetrator arguing with the statue of King Richard shortly before its disappearance, and then their joint reappearance later roaring up and down Westminster Bridge aboard Boudicca's chariot in the company of fierce Boudicca AND her two daughters. Apparently this news was all over the place and yet the authorities were peculiarly unforthcoming as to the perpetrator's identity or any details pertaining to the case.

The consensus among the witnesses was that the perpetrator reminded them of the mythic figure of Britannia. Little realizing how apt her words would prove to be, Juliet commented that the details were bound to turn up on the Internet, if they weren't all over it already.

The strange nervousness in Stewart's stomach only increased when he heard others describing some crazy young bloke who played leapfrog from rooftop to rooftop, pausing only to sit atop chimneys and make faces at the police before disappearing completely. And good riddance to him was the general opinion. It wasn't the stranger's improbably antics that unsettled Stewart so much as the distinct description of his cap: a blue baseball cap embroidered with gleaming golden wings. It was all too familiar.

The feeling intensified when Stewart overheard two of Juliet's old girlfriends talking about the flaming loon who called himself the 'Vampire of Love' and chased women all over the place last night. They described the stranger as being handsome enough, but an absolute nutter, or perhaps only as high as a kite? In the end, it made no difference in their estimations. The police chased him up onto the rooftops too and eventually lost track of him as well. If he made a return appearance that night, quite a few men swore to give him the beating he deserved for terrorizing their girlfriends.

As they moved on, Juliet commented, " 'Sounds as though the police had a busy night of it, doesn't it, Stew?"

" 'Sounds like everyone did," he said.

"Except us." Juliet took on a mock pout. "We missed all the excitement."

"Thank God for small favors," Stewart muttered.

In the grocers, they overheard Mrs. Nesbit bemoaning the sudden absence of her marmalade cat to Mrs. Gupta, who didn't help matters one bit when she claimed to have glimpsed a large python with glowing orange eyes slithering along the tops of the fences several houses down and heading in the direction of Mrs. Nesbit's house.

"I'll have to warn, Mum," said Juliet. "It'd be awful if Nacho got swallowed up."

Stewart spent the next two hours with Juliet trying to delay the inevitable: going home.

6. Saturday Morning at the Dunks'

Udela stood staring over her fence at the rumpled lump that was Hermes, sprawled atop the picnic table with his head buried beneath his arms and jacket. At every odd moment, a groan or a moan escaped him. Rather like a sleeping hound, a flinch or a kick usually accompanied the sounds he emitted, and despite the little noises she made against the fence he did not wake up.

Another, deeper groan betrayed Marshall's presence beneath the picnic table.

Udela craned, strained and bent until she could just see his feet sticking out from beneath. She smiled and flicked her refreshed blonde hair past her ear. "Marshall? Is that you?" she called.

Mars' feet stirred and shifted, and then withdrew from sight. He peered out. "Morning." The sound of his own voice caused him to hold his head for a moment.

"'Made a night of it, did we?" she said.

Mars winced at every simpering syllable rolling out of her rouged lips. Her ultra-bright clothing caused him to squint and cringe away. "It would seem so. I just don't remember crawling under here." Spying Hermes' foot hanging over the edge, he tapped at Hermes' foot. "Hey, Hermes. Do you remember how I got under here?"

Hermes groaned and yanked his foot out of reach.

"I think you're more likely to get an answer out of this fence than you will your friend," said Udela.

"Oh?" Mars hauled himself out for a look. "Oh." He smacked Hermes in the foot again.

"I don't make house calls," Hermes mumbled as he burrowed deeper under his jacket.

"Get up, you lazy sot." Mars smacked him with his own baseball cap.

Hermes yelped and rolled off the table. Sitting in a heap, he rubbed his head and, yanking down his jacket, glared up at Mars. Up bobbed a very firm pair of donkey ears, gray in color.

For a moment, Mars stared in bedazzled astonishment. Then the God of War doubled over in an insane fit of unseemly and uncharacteristic giggling.

Udela clapped her hands together though. "Oh! I didn't realize that there was a production of 'A Midsummer Night's Dream' going on."

Hermes blinked up at Udela. He rubbed his eyes. She looked like a paint explosion. "What?"

Mars stood grinning. "Actually it was more like one of those reality shows, right, Hermes?"

"You must be playing 'Bottom'," Udela prattled on.

Mars snorted and covered his mouth.

Hermes frowned at Mars. "What is she burbling about?"

Mars was enjoying the situation too much to enlighten him. "Staying in costume so he could stay in character, that's dedication for you, eh, Mrs. Dunk?"

She nodded, "That's method acting for you. Recite a few lines."

"Lines?" said Hermes.

Mars kicked him in the foot. "You heard her. Recite some of the Immortal Bard."

"Sod off." Flinging himself to his feet, Hermes

stomped inside.

Mars sighed and shook his head. "I guess the rehearsal went badly."

" 'Must have," said Udela. Her gaze brightened anew as it settled upon Marshall and his tall, athletic physique.

Of course, Mars noticed her close, drooling scrutiny, but he had one ear primed toward the house.

Udela's mind returned to the concern at hand. "I do expect you and your friends promptly at ten," then she added with a curling tone, "but I'm perfectly willing to give YOU a personal 'VIP' tour."

Mars tensed just a little. "Never fear. WE will be there."

She sighed. "Very well, but if you change your mind…" She started to turn away, but stopped. "By the way, did Stewart stay with you and your friends last night?"

"He left without having so much as one spoon of stew."

Twisting her mouth, Udela grunted and went inside her house.

A startled shriek erupted then from the abode of the Gods. Mars grinned. There was another cry. This one sounded more wretched. It was something akin to a howl. He chuckled.

Out staggered Hermes. Each hand tugged at a long furry gray ear. Behind him crept wide-eyed Venus, with her hands pressed to her mouth.

More incoherent than not, half-formed words tumbled out of Hermes' mouth. Then his eyes rolled back into his head and he fainted into Mars's arms. Mars burst out laughing and dropped him.

"Ares!" cried Venus.

"I'm sorry, but – look at him!" He bent over in another spasm of laughter.

Medusa eased through the gate. Using the fence to keep from veering desperately off course, she measured her steps, but with every odd step, she made a face and paused to hack and cough before she resuming her progress toward the picnic table.

At that moment Hermes sat up, a woebegone expression firmly fixed upon his face, which he turned toward Medusa in hopes of gaining some sympathy.

Medusa took one look and doubled over laughing, until another fit of coughing struck her.

Hermes stood up, and laying back his wondrous great gray ears, stomped into the house – just as Athena shuffled out.

Athena recoiled and sprung aside. "What the - ?"

"NOT ONE WORD." Hermes thrust a commanding finger into her face as he slipped past her.

Athena covered her sudden smile with her hand and came the rest of the way outside. Just as it had Medusa, the picnic table with its sturdy benches drew her on with the urgency of a life raft upon the rolling ocean. As soon as she felt the table beneath her hands, Athena settled onto a bench and pressed both hands to her head. She jerked her thumb toward their back door. "What happened to him?"

"Methinks he ran mightily afoul of my Lord Oberon last night," said Mars.

"Oh, well, that explains it."

Medusa had another spasm of hacking and coughing.

Athena took on a genuine frown of concern. "Are you all right?"

"There's a tickle in my throat," said Medusa in a

throatier voice then usual.

"Be careful or you'll cough up a lung," said Athena.

"Well, if I do, Apollo can fix it. He knows the best physicians."

"You two look like Hell warmed over," said Mars.

Athena pointed her finger. "That's a lovely shiner you got there too, Mars. I really like that particular shade of bluish purple."

"Shiner?" He reached up and winced as his fingers touched his black eye. "Ouch."

Medusa whistled. "That's a beaut! What DID you do last night?"

"I don't remember - not exactly."

"Try," said Athena.

"Well, when I roared out of here last night, I remember stopping off in India to pick up Kali. Then the two of us went to Rio." Gingerly, Mars prodded at his black eye again. "It's all a psychedelic blur after that."

Medusa's eyes widened. "You were with Kali?"

"Yes."

Medusa clapped her hands. "I gotta hand it to you – hanging out with Kali in Rio. You're one serious bad ass."

Athena nodded. "That is impressive."

"Kali?" said Venus in a tone that made Mars wince. He had forgotten that she was standing behind him. "You went to Rio with Kali? Did you stop off for Margueritas with Pele on the way?"

Mars' eyes widened. "Actually, now that I think about it…."

"Look," Venus held up her hands, "dear. I don't know where all you went last night and I don't care to know, but I do know where you'll be tonight:

Couchville."

"That will certainly be an improvement over sleeping under the picnic table," Mars grumbled.

"Is that where you woke up?" said Venus.

"Yes."

"Why?"

"I don't remember. The last thing I do remember with absolute clarity is sitting at this table eating that infernal stew of yours."

Venus folded her arms across her breast. "You said you liked it."

"And I did, but I think those mushrooms you used were a little 'off'."

Resigned to his condition, Hermes slumped back out, toast in one hand and coffee cup in the other. "Those were 'Special' Mushrooms." He arched his brow for further emphasis. "I couldn't simply pop over to the market and buy them. Nooo. I had to fly all over the bloody planet to hand pick the buggers."

"The Delphic Oracle's recipe was quite specific," Venus insisted.

"Well, next time just send Hermes to Harrods or to a gourmet market in Paris. What we had last night was a little 'rich' to put it politely," said Mars.

Hermes bent down for a closer look at Medusa. "Is that cat fur on your clothes, Medusa?"

"Yes." She wrinkled her nose. "I woke up in a tunnel covered with it. I can't seem to get it out of my mouth either."

"But why are you covered in it?" said Hermes. Medusa shrugged.

Udela marched outside. Impatience made her brisk. Jealousy caused her to narrow her gaze at Venus. "It is nearly ten. Are you and your friends coming over or not?"

"I'm missing a man. As soon as I find him, Mrs. Dunk, we'll come 'round." Mars mouthed to the rest, 'Where is he?'

The others exchanged bleary-eyed looks and shrugged.

Reluctantly, Udela began to turn back, but stopped. "You might as well keep an eye out. Mrs. Nesbit's cat has gone missing."

Medusa went stark staring rigid. Except for Udela, they all noticed.

"Oh?" said Mars.

Hermes plucked some of the fur off of Medusa's shirt. "What color was it?"

"Orange marmalade, like that cat in the comics," said Udela.

A wicked grin spread across Hermes' face as he shook the fur in Medusa's face.

Udela peered under her shrubs. "Mrs. Nesbit is very attached to that cat. Her daughter gave it to her as a kitten."

Medusa groaned and buried her face on her arms.

Udela gave up her little search. "Oh well. I'll be seeing you shortly, Mr. Marshall." She gave him a meaningful look which he barely responded to, and went back inside

Medusa raised her head. She looked thoroughly disgusted with herself.

Hermes shook his head. "I hope you're proud of yourself."

Medusa grimaced like one afflicted with a fresh hangover. "Shut it, Hermes," she groused.

Athena managed to be sympathetic, up to a point. "You had that snake dream again, didn't you?"

"I ate an old lady's cat. I'm going straight to Hell."

"Excuse me? The snake dream?" said Mars.

Medusa sighed. "I have these dreams in which I'm either grappling with a snake in a tunnel…"

Hermes snorted and grinned.

Medusa gave him a warning glance. "…or I am the snake in the tunnel."

Mars stroked his chin. "Hmmmm…I wonder what Freud would make of that?"

Medusa's eyes turned diamond hard. Her locks and braids writhed within the red bandanna. "Do NOT start with me. Not today."

Although that shut them both up, the two Gods still smirked.

After a quick peek outside, Erian strode outside armed with a smug grin and several freshly printed sheets of paper.

Mars sighed and scanned the horizons. "Does anyone know where Apollo…" Spotting Erian across the fence listening to every word, Mars added, "I mean, Phoebus is?"

"Perhaps I can help you there," said Erian.

"Oh? Did you see Phoebus?" said Athena.

" 'Phoebus'? Last night? Yes." The way he drew out 'Yessss' gave them all pause.

"All right then. Tell us. What was he doing?" said Hermes. When the others looked at him, he shrugged. " 'Might as well get it over with."

"Actually for all I know he could be in police custody, sleeping it off, but when I saw him, he was chasing birds up and down the street."

"Birds?" Hermes glanced skyward. "At night? Wouldn't he be chasing bats instead?"

Athena, Medusa and Venus chorused, "GIRLS."

"Oh!" Hermes grinned impishly.

Erian went on. "I tried to stop him and talk to him, but all he kept saying was that he was the Vampire of Love and needed brides."

Mars started laughing.

Hermes would have laughed, but suddenly he stood up.

"What's wrong?" said Venus.

"Nothing." He winked over his shoulder. "Just a hunch." Hermes walked around toward a side door, the one that connected with a room that had been converted into a bomb shelter during the War and then into a work shed. He yanked the door open.

Out flopped Apollo in a groaning lump.

"Found him." Hermes returned to the table and his coffee.

Mars walked over, leaned down, took a deep breath, and…"RISE AND SHINE!"

Apollo flung his arms over his head and writhed.

Mars ambled back toward the picnic table. "Now he's up."

Apollo propped himself up and scowled at him.

Wearing an almost unbearably bright smile, Venus called out, "Morning, Phoebus! Would you like tea or coffee?"

Apollo cocked a frown at her. "Normal tea or some scary Delphic brew?"

"Store bought! Honestly – !"

"Tea would be fine."

"Tea then." Venus narrowed her eyes at him, but went in.

Apollo crawled across the yard and up onto the bench, where he settled with a groan next to Athena.

"Does anyone have a mint?"

"Why?" said Athena.

"Can't you smell it?" Medusa waved her hand before her nose and made a face. "Pee-eww!"

Apollo held his hand over his mouth. "I think she put too much garlic in that stew."

Mars's face lit up again. "If only poor Daphne had been armed with garlic – ."

Apollo glared. "You would bring her up."

"Do you remember anything at all about last night?" said Mars.

Apollo glanced quickly at Erian, who was being much too attentive. "No, do you?"

"More than you apparently." Mars folded his arms across his chest and shook his head at the rumpled Sun God.

"What are you smirking at?"

Mars adopted a mock French accent. "You – the Vampire of Love."

Apollo suffered a prolonged, excruciating moment of crystal clear realization. Naturally, his eyes shot wide open. "Oh – no."

"I'd lay low for a few weeks," commented Erian. "You don't have just the police looking for you."

Although she covered her mouth, Athena's laugh escaped anyway, which she regretted instantly for the fresh pain it inflicted. She pressed her hand to her forehead.

"Oh. Ha ha," went Apollo. "How come your robes are so damp? And your sandals are soaking wet too? What did you get up to last night?"

Athena frowned. "I'm not quite sure I can remember. My head…" She buried her face in her hands.

"Perhaps I can help you there. I pulled this from the internet news service." As he read, Erian gave them all cunning looks. "'Full Moon Produces Strange Sightings and Improbable Thefts. This morning the British public awoke to discover that overnight someone had made off not only with the statue of Richard the Lionheart, which stood guard outside the Houses of Parliament, but also the statues of Boudicca and her daughters, complete with their chariot.'"

Athena's head shot up. Her eyes stared.

"And the fog lifts," said Apollo.

Erian continued, "'Alarming as these thefts were, what is much more peculiar are the sightings various individuals reported of an inebriated woman clad in archaic Grecian robes shouting at the statue of Richard the Lionheart. Later, observers also claim to have seen the same woman racing back and forth across the bridge in a chariot accompanied by three equally fierce, Celtic looking women. Miraculously as it was nearly three in the morning no one was hurt.'"

Watching Athena closely, he let that sink in a moment, before continuing. "There's a bit more. 'At about four in the morning, a woman fitting the same description was seen wading down the center of the Thames.' There were witnesses. Images were taken. Video footage too." Erian held up a full color print of an only slightly fuzzy, but unmistakable image of Athena in full Grecian attire complete with her helmet, breastplate, and spear. He waved a computer disc. "I burned a copy of the footage."

"Ohhhhh God." Athena buried her face in her hands.

"God died laughing," said Medusa.

"Medusa?" said Mars.

"What?"

"Meee-oww!"

Medusa cringed and flicked her tongue against her teeth again.

Erian sized them all up again. "So who are you people really?"

"I don't know," said Apollo, "but you seem to have it all figured out, so why don't you tell us?"

"Well, at first, I just had my suspicions. Your names rankled. I'm not deaf. Minerva, Medusa, Phoebus, 'Herman', Ares or Mars. I'm not blind either. There's something odd about you, especially the bird with the wriggly hair."

Medusa adjusted her bandanna with a sulking look.

Affecting nonchalance, Mars folded his arms across his chest. "So we're a bunch of nutters, so what?"

"I might have accepted that," Erian held up the printouts, "but then 'Minerva' went on her little escapade. I'm not stupid. Improbable as it may be, I know who you are. What I haven't figured out is why you're here."

Medusa glared. "Don't ask any questions you don't want the answers to."

Erian met her gaze rather brazenly for a mere mortal. "Still, one wonders what the authorities would do if someone told them where to find the mystery lady last seen striding dead center down the Thames?"

Athena peered round Apollo and Medusa at him. "What do you suppose your mother would say if her boy genius turned into a babbling idiot overnight?"

Erian blanched and backed off fast. "I was only teasing."

"I'm watching you, boy," snarled Athena.

Erian retreated into the house.

Apollo nudged Athena. "Actually that would be an idea."

"What would?" said Hermes.

Apollo arched his brows at Athena. "Letting Erian tell the authorities." He whistled and circled his finger beside his brow.

Athena slammed her fist on the table. "Brilliant."

Venus came out with Apollo's tea. "Here! Plain tea. No breakfast tea though. All I had was afternoon tea." She set it before Apollo and gave him a little curtsey.

Apollo saluted her with his cup and took a long recuperative sip.

All attention reverted to Athena and remained there.

"What?" Athena squirmed.

Mars prodded her. "All right. Let's hear it."

Athena rubbed her brow and, now that she remembered last night in all its surreal details, began, "I was strolling past the Houses of Parliament, thinking I'd go pay my respects at the tomb of Queen Elizabeth the First when I thought I heard the statue of Richard Lionheart say something insulting about women in battle gear. Naturally, I walked directly over and gave him a piece of my mind."

Mars raised his hand. "Let me get this straight: You were yelling at a statue?"

"I thought he was alive."

"You didn't realize that it was a statue?"

"I did - eventually."

"And?" said Hermes.

"I couldn't talk to him if he was a statue, so I brought him to life."

Collectively, the cry went up. "You what?!"

Athena cringed. "I brought him to life so we could finish our argument."

Apollo began chuckling.

Athena prodded him, but it did nothing to stifle his mirth. "Despite the fact that while on a crusade his own mother rode like an Amazon and that I myself was a divine entity with a firm grasp of military strategy and more than a little experience in warfare, Richard Lionheart continued to mock the very idea of a woman in a position of leadership, so I brought Boudicca's statue to life too."

Athena looked around at all the shocked looks turned her way. "I had to! Boudicca was a war chieftain. It made sense to bring her into the debate – or so it seemed at the time."

Mars' grin had spread from ear to ear. "What happened next?"

Athena sighed and rubbed her forehead. "Boudicca thought Richard was with the Romans. You know, all that armor… I had to fight to keep her from trying to kill him."

"Two statues smashing each other to bits – I'd pay to see that," said Hermes.

"At last they came to an understanding," said Athena.

"What sort of understanding?" said Mars.

Athena bit her lip.

"Athena?" said Apollo.

"I sent them on a crusade."

"Where?" said Medusa.

"Athena?" said Apollo.

"Antioch, I think."

"You sent them to Turkey?!" shouted Mars.

The rest came out in a breathless rush. "Not right

away. First I brought Boudicca's girls to life and restored their chariot – and off we all went."

"Where do you suppose they are now?" said Apollo with a glance at Mars.

"On their way to pick up Joan of Arc – and then it's off to Antioch. But don't worry," said Athena.

Apollo and Mars gaped at her.

She added quickly, "I don't think they'll get any further than Dover."

"What if they take the Chunnel?" said Medusa.

"They'll be smashed to pieces, that is IF they didn't revert to their original forms again when the sun came up."

Mars gave Athena a long meaningful look.

Athena sighed and headed for the gate. "I'll go find them and fix everything." She set off down the sidewalk, scattering grumbles in her wake.

Mars jogged Apollo in the shoulder. "Ready to go to work?"

"Work?"

"The renovations at the Dunk house, Nosferatu."

"Oh. Yeah." Apollo chortled fiendishly, but as he stood up, his gaze fell upon Hermes, who sat with his head in his hands and a woe-is-me look on his face. "We really should do something about those ears of yours, Hermes."

Hermes perked up. "Do you know a spell?"

"A spell?" Mars snorted. "Who needs spells? A snip here and a snip there and you'll be your old self."

Hermes grabbed his ears. "Surgery?"

"More like pruning actually," said Mars.

"Will you be doing it for me, Apollo?" said Hermes.

"I think Mars wants to do it."

Mars took on a fearsome smile. "Let me go find the scissors."

Hermes jumped up. "Huh-uh!" He backed toward the gate. "No way!" Then he darted out of it.

"Apollo," said Mars.

Apollo gulped down the last of his tea and smacked his lips. "I'll get him." He sauntered out the gate and strolled down the sidewalk. "Come here, you big baby."

Rubbing his hands together, Mars went in. The low chuckle that escaped him was disturbing.

"I don't think I want to see this," said Venus.

"I do," said Medusa.

Moving out of harm's way, Venus and Medusa leaned against the fence.

Aiken peeked out the window. His face lit up and he dropped the curtain again.

Hermes ran past down the sidewalk.

A moment later, Apollo strolled past after him. "You're only making things harder on yourself."

Aiken crept out of his back door, up to Venus and leaned over the fence just far enough to plant a kiss on her neck. "Mornin', love."

Venus jumped so high and with such loud violence that both Aiken and Medusa leapt away from her.

For a long moment, Venus stood with her hand pressed to her heart until her breath calmed somewhat. Her wide-eyed gaze did not move from Aiken's grinning face. She scolded him, "You frightened the daylights out of me."

"Sorry, sweetheart, but I couldn't resist another little peck."

"Well, next time – resist."

"Another?" said Medusa.

Venus frowned. "See? You gave me the hiccups."

"Come here, I've got just the cure you need." Aiken reached for her.

"I'll settle for a glass of water." Venus began to turn away.

"I missed you when I woke up this morning."

Venus froze.

Medusa clapped her hand over her mouth. This was too good to be true.

Venus turned back around. "I'm sorry?"

Aiken leered. "We had such a rollicking good time, didn't we? So naturally I was a little surprised to roll over and find myself alone."

It dawned on her. "Oh NO."

"Oh, yes, four times. It was fucking amazing."

"Or amazing fucking," said Medusa.

Venus swiped at her. Medusa ducked and posted herself on the far side of the picnic table, a perfect spot to watch.

Aiken mock-sulked. "I thought we had something special."

Medusa couldn't resist. "Oh, you had something special all right."

"Medusa," cried Venus.

Medusa chortled. "After all, she is the bloody Goddess of Love."

"She what?" A frown glanced across his brow.

Venus stretched out the syllables into a growl. "Medusa."

Medusa was enjoying herself too much. "So the sex had better be mind-blowing! Right?"

Aiken's gaze lingered admiringly upon Venus and her delicious curves. "I'll say. A lot more than my mind got blown last night." He winked.

"Ewww!" Medusa wrinkled her nose. "That's a mental image I could've done without. Yuck."

Aiken caught a hold of Venus' left hand and took to caressing it. "So, when are you going to break the news to your ex?"

"My ex?"

"Yeah, that Marshall bloke."

Medusa piped up. "Yes, Venus dear, have you told Mar-shall about this?"

Venus smiled ever so sweetly. "Medusa dear?"

"Yes?"

"Meee-ow."

"Damn you." Medusa started for the gate. "Hey, Aiken, you wouldn't know where one can find an orange marmalade kitten on short notice?" But he was too busy mooning over Venus to reply. "I thought not," she mumbled.

Just as she set foot on the sidewalk, Hermes came barreling towards her. Medusa stopped and, laid a hand on the knot restraining her coiling braids and rattled. Nearly losing his balance, Hermes squeaked past her and stumbled off.

As Medusa passed from sight, Apollo walked swiftly into view. "Come on. It won't hurt long. Snip-snip and you'll be your old self again." Then he passed from sight again with his hands shoved into his pockets.

"So when are you going to tell him?" Aiken said.

"Tell him what?" said Venus without a trace of her usual charm.

"About us?"

Venus yanked her hand free. "There is no 'us'."

"You're breaking my heart."

"Oh? You have one to break after all? Aiken, listen carefully. What we had was a one-night stand.

You know what those are, right? You've inflicted enough of them on others. Think of it this way: Now, you know how it feels."

Half-mortified, Aiken half-teased, "You're horrible. You know that."

"Oh, boo-hoo. Trust me, I can be worse. Now, go and play."

"You can't mean this." Now he was in a sulk.

"What! You think you're God's gift to women? This can't happen to little ol' you?"

"There isn't a woman who's been with me and regretted it."

"Oh really?" Venus pivoted toward him. Her head bobbed and a cutting smile curled upon her lips as she set her hands on her hips. "Very well."

She blew a kiss at him and for a moment he felt something akin to a whirlwind spin over him, and then stillness settled upon him. The birds in the shrubbery though made a frantic racket.

"Congratulations, Stud, now you're absolutely irresistible to women."

"Yeah, right." Aiken began to grin, but hesitated under her cold smile. "No? Really?"

"Go for a little stroll. I dare you."

For once in his life, Aiken felt utterly uncertain. "You're just saying that."

"Am I? There's but one way to find out: Open the gate and take a little stroll. Go on. Now, put your foot out."

"Oh, stop it. I'm going. Nothing's going to happen though"

Aiken opened his gate, just as Hermes came darting by. There sounded a solid thwack, or it might have been a thunk, followed by an equally solid thud on the sidewalk.

"Thank you, Aiken." Apollo arrived, rubbed his hands together and seized a hold of Hermes.

Hermes began flailing about. "No! No, you don't."

Apollo wasn't having any of it. "Come on. Be a man. It won't hurt for long."

Before he realized it, Aiken was out on the sidewalk as Apollo pinned Hermes' arm behind his back and propelled him through the gaping gate.

Mars chose that moment to step outside. Over his work clothes he wore his kitchen apron – complete with a crude chef's greeting printed over the images of two fried eggs, sunny side up of course – and a red bandanna on his head. In one hand he held a long pair of scissors that gleamed especially bright from being freshly sharpened and in the other hand bobbed a steak mallet. He raised the scissors. Snip, snap they went as he grinned. "Two clips and you'll be your old bloody worthless self again.

"The Hell I will!" Hermes bucked and kicked, but his doom was assured the moment Mars grabbed him by the collar.

Apollo let him go and sauntered behind as Mars dragged Hermes in the rest of the way. Aiken would have sworn he heard Apollo chuckling.

"Wait a minute! What about the anesthetic?" said Hermes.

"That's what the mallet's for," said Mars.

The back door closed behind them.

From within the house, a brief scuffle erupted.

"Mommy! Mommy!"

"Sit on him, Apollo," said Mars.

"Don't you bite me," yelled Apollo. "If you bite

me, we'll give your ears a Van Gogh bob."

"Still now….", said Mars.

A sudden, nervous silence engulfed the house. Then Venus and Aiken heard the scissors snap - twice in swift succession.

Two seconds later, Hermes hurtled outside with his hands clasped over his offending and offended ears.

His tormentors followed him outside.

Instead of the mallet and scissors, Mars dangled the donkey ears from his hands. "See? No harm done, you big baby."

Hermes uncovered his ears. They looked normal once more.

"Next time, stay clear of Titania before Oberon does worse to you," said Apollo.

Mars pulled off his apron and threw it at Hermes. "Change into your work clothes. We've got a job to do."

His bottom lip jutting out, Hermes stomped past him back inside. He cast stormy looks at Mars.

"Hurry up. We're late as it is," snapped Mars, but he was smiling. He even waved when he saw Udela peek out the kitchen window at him.

Venus turned her head toward the sidewalk. "What? Are you still here?" She waved Aiken on. "Take a turn around the block and see what happens."

"I'll be back. You be ready for me." Aiken exchanged looks with Mars, cocksure of his ascendancy in Venus' favor, and set off whistling some raffish Tom Jones' melody.

"Aphrodite?" said Mars "Darling, what was that about?"

"Nothing." Venus sighed and trudged past him into the house, "Except, that's the last time I make mushroom stew."

"Where are you going?"

"To scrub myself with sandpaper."

Hermes came back out and suffered Apollo to thrust him out the gate toward the Dunks' house where Udela had emerged, her eager face bright with impatience and fresh rouge, but still not as bright as her clothes.

7. The Tour

From what Mars, Apollo and Hermes could tell, Udela was something of an obsessive when it came to cleanliness and order. She made them wipe their feet the instant they came in the back door. After Hermes idly twirled her ashtray atop the counter top with his index finger, she removed it abruptly from his reach and set it back precisely where it belonged, with a firm little tap. She gave Hermes a cool, commanding look before turning again with her bright, glossy red smile towards Mars, who had been exchanging significant looks with Apollo.

Udela had moved on, prattling on about how she didn't like her cabinets and describing some more maniacally elaborate design that she wanted to a mute, goggle-eyed Hermes.

Meanwhile, Apollo shrugged at Mars, whispering, "It makes perfect sense in a perverse way: her life is a wreck, so everything around her must be micromanaged just so for her to be happy. Deep down she recognizes that she herself is viewed as something distasteful and improper, so her physical surroundings must be beyond reproach to the casual eye, even if to her own dubious standards." He cocked his brow for emphasis at the colors in the kitchen. "Day-Glo lime green and fluorescent orange polka dots – not a good combination." Sage-like, he nodded to himself. "Yes, Sir-eee, it all comes down to toxic egotism."

Mars rubbed the space between his eyes and squeezed his eyes closed a moment. "Whatever it is – it's hurting my eyes."

"Frankly, this kitchen looks exactly the same as it did when Mr. Dunk and little Aiken and myself moved in," Udela was saying as she laughed. "It's stuck in the 70's." She sighed from so much self-induced mirth and motioned toward the doorway. "The dining room is this way."

Apollo observed the keen electric glance Udela lavished upon Mars as she passed him and the way her hand brushed his brawny arm.

"The kitchen isn't the only thing stuck in the 70's," grumbled Mars. "The woman's pushing 60 and she's carrying on like she's still 25."

Still the sage, Apollo nodded, "Colossal egotism. Don't say you weren't warned."

"Warned of what?" said Mars as he brought up the rear.

After the kitchen's time warp, the dining room and living room came as something of a surprise – initially. There were some agreeably lovely old objects arranged in disagreeably crowded and yet still obsessive order: Udela's prized hoard. Apparently, when she wasn't chasing down a good time, she was hunting down treasures to delight her eyes. She had a good eye for value, if one judged by the trophies she pointed out.

It became apparent also that no one lived in the living room or dared to trespass in the dining room either, except with Udela's permission. Apollo could not detect even the ghost of a fingerprint anywhere on the polished oak table in the center of the room and the glare that Udela fixed on Hermes guaranteed that his idle fingers did not stroll across it either.

Erian thumped downstairs. In his hands, he held the incriminating printouts, but he stopped when he saw who was there. "Mum?"

Udela turned stern and forbidding in an instant. "What?"

He eyed the three Gods, felt their wolfish stares boring through him, and shrugged. "Nothing. It can wait." Giving Apollo a lingering look of distrust, he shuffled toward the kitchen.

They heard him snap on the radio in the kitchen and open and close cabinets, but as soon as his mother resumed speaking to her visitors, he turned the volume way down low.

"I'm sure he'll tell us what else he has on his mind when he's good and ready," muttered Apollo to Mars.

Udela stood in the doorway motioning them onward toward the front hall. "If you're ready, we'll resume."

Hermes slipped past her as though afraid that she would swat him if he lingered too close.

Apollo was still casting a dubious look back at Udela's shrine to selfishness that was the living room as he shuffled past her.

Mars was the last. Their eyes locked. Udela's smile took on a look of greedy feline avarice. He averted his gaze. It landed on Apollo and Hermes who gazed back as Mars moved past her. They saw Mars flinch and give a slight, astonished spring forward as Udela's smile sharpened.

Udela moved to follow.

Mars moved in two swift, broad steps behind Apollo and Hermes, well out of her reach.

Opening the front door, she motioned for them to come for a look.

"Watch out, Ares," whispered Hermes with a keen grin. "She's got the hots for you."

As could be expected, Mars retaliated.

"Ow! My head. Hey! Don't shove."

"I'm sorry, Mrs. Dunk," said Mars most charmingly. "What was that you were saying about your front door?"

"It needs fixing. It sticks. See? It doesn't open as readily as it should."

"That's probably because it's been opening and closing a little too often, if you know what I mean," smirked Hermes. "Ow!"

"...and perhaps a new splash of color when you're done with it?" continued Udela, oblivious, or rather, indifferent to why two of the men were grinning while the third scowled and rubbed the back of his head.

"How about red?" said Hermes. "Ow! Quit it, Mars."

"Blue would be nice," she said as she came back inside. The look she gave Hermes would have turned the Fountain of Youth to dust. "Now, if you'll follow me upstairs."

Mars made certain that Hermes and Apollo preceded him.

Glancing back, Apollo noticed Erian narrowing his eyes at them from the kitchen doorway.

Their first stop was Aiken's room, a perfect shrine to his male vanity. Therefore, it had to be redone completely, starting with a lovely lavender coat of paint, once all of his posters and rubbish had been taken away of course.

Her three would be laborers exchanged quiet looks of dismayed astonishment.

As soon as she stepped out, motioning them all

the while to follow her to Erian's haven, Hermes mumbled, "And here I thought Aiken was her favorite."

"He is," said Apollo, "or she'd have him painted lavender too."

They followed her again only as far as Erian's personal threshold and peered in.

Udela wore a look of uncomprehending boredom as she surveyed Erian's wall of book and his precious electronics. His computer was already on and they could just see the news bulletin on the screen. What they glimpsed had them so riveted for a moment that they didn't hear what Udela was saying.

"...Erian will have a fit if I do away with his junk, so I was thinking of having you build him a cabinet to house all of this...mess. I would like it painted in a nice French Provencal style. Powder blue should do for this room, I think, especially once we get his bric a brac and posters off of the wall."

Hermes chewed on his bottom lip and shook his head, and continued to do so even as she fixed a hard look on him in passing. Then his gaze returned to that computer screen. His eyes had not lied and neither had Erian. Although the image was not the best, the video image replaying on the screen was, unmistakably, Athena on her now infamous spree. Apollo gave him a meaningful look as he closed Erian's bedroom door before Udela actually got a good look at the screen.

Mars fidgeted outside Stewart's room, keeping a safe distance from Udela while she struggled with Stewart's doorknob.

"Looks like it's locked," Mars said at last.

Udela bit her lip and smacked Stewart's door with the palm of her hand. "We'll come back to it later. We'll look at my room next." Her hand passed firmly atop

Mars' arm as she passed him.

Mars grimaced and managed not to recoil. Then he mumbled to the other two, "Smart man that Stewart — he locks his bedroom door."

"That's probably so he won't come home and find that she's moved him out onto the curb," said Hermes very lowly.

"She wouldn't do that," said Apollo just as lowly. "She needs him and Erian for their paychecks."

With a flourish and a seductive smile, Udela opened her bedroom door and went in, hips swaying. "Red. I want a flaming-crimson-red bedroom."

They re-grouped in the doorway to Udela's leopard-spotted orange and black boudoir.

As soon as he got an eyeful, Apollo said, "Why does this not surprise me?"

Hermes flinched. "I blame Disco."

"Me too," said Mars.

"…with lots of pillows," said Udela.

"What is it with women and pillows?" Mars muttered.

Hermes and Apollo shrugged.

"This can go. That can go. I want this moved over there…"

"And everything turned inside out and upside down," mimicked Hermes under his breath.

Apollo nudged him silent, but he was smirking too.

Mars glanced at her list. "Is that it?"

Udela paused and, confounded for a moment, she looked about herself. "Yes. I think so. Yes."

"Ohhh-kay," said Mars, turning away with his attention still on the list.

Eager to be far away from Udela's den of iniquity,

Apollo sped downstairs. Hands in pockets, Hermes sauntered lazily after him.

Mars turned to follow.

"Oh! I forgot the bathroom," she said. "There's a problem with the plumbing. You'd better have a look."

Mars sighed. "All right." The plumbing was on the list. He pivoted and turned back.

Udela stood beside the bathroom sink and peered beneath it intently. "It drips a bit," she said as he joined her.

Mars stooped over for a look. "Are you sure about a leak, Mrs. Dunk?" he was saying as he frowned and touched the drainpipe. It was dry.

Udela slipped around him back into the doorway.

Mars went rigid. There was no mistaking it. That was Udela's hand idling most admiringly along his right shoulder and then traveling with languorous, but firm intent all the way down his back and to his behind, which she gave an appreciative and expert smack with the palm of her hand. He stood up and stepped back, but didn't get far, not with the bathroom wall standing so conveniently close.

Udela pressed her overripe body close and let her equally overripe perfume saturate his senses. "Are you sure the pipes couldn't use a little 'adjusting'?"

The sound Mars heard was his zipper – heading south with purposeful deliberation. Somehow she'd already un-did the button on his jeans without him feeling it. "The pipes were fine last I looked," he said.

Udela looked down. "Mmmm. They certainly are – or rather, IT is."

"Uhhh. I think I hear my girlfriend calling me."

"She's had her fun, had it all night with my son Aiken," Udela's tone briefly stooped into raspy irritation.

" 'Quite ruined my beauty sleep with the noise they made, and that's after she ruined my evening. My date took one look at her crawling all over my son on my sofa, where they shouldn't have been in the first place, and couldn't tear his eyes from her. He just sat on the end of my bed listening to the noise they made, until I had to give him the boot. NOW IT'S MY TURN."

Mars glanced out through the doorway. From the end of the hall, he saw Hermes grinning around the corner back at him. "My friends will be wondering…"

Udela glanced, but Hermes' grinning face ducked back into the stairwell.

"They won't be wondering for long," she said.

"Uhhh…OH! That's quite a grip you have, Mrs. Dunk."

"Call me Udela." Her tone deepened even as she sank to her knees.

"Ohhh-kaay, Udela. Whoa! Ohh. Wow!"

Apollo had gone nearly all the way to the back door when he realized that he was alone. Ignoring the crafty look Erian gave him from the stove, where he prodded at some sausages sizzling loudly in the skillet, Apollo ventured back toward the stairs. The instant he poked his head around the corner he spied Hermes sitting just below the landing smiling hugely toward the bathroom.

"What are you doing?"

Hermes pressed his finger to his grinning mouth and gestured around the corner.

Apollo hadn't taken two steps up when he heard a small, but fierce, furtive scuffle and then a bump and another. The bumping had a distinctive rhythm to it. He stopped right where he was, a sickened look on his face.

"Ummmm," went Udela. "Yes. Oh yes! I knew

it! Give it – Harder. Harder!"

"Oh yeah. YEAH!"

Hermes covered his mouth so they wouldn't hear
the laughter that doubled him over where he sat and sent
tears down his cheeks.

Apollo shook his head in horrified disbelief.

Downstairs Erian turned up the radio – loud.

Hermes bobbed his head and wiped the tears from
his cheeks, which only worsened when he saw the face
that Apollo made. Helpless, he crumpled over on the
top steps.

"Yes! YES!" Udela let go a deep-throated animal
cry and gasped.

Mars let go a picturesque little roar of his own.

Hermes peered 'round again.

"He's going to kill you if he catches you peeking,"
Apollo hissed.

Hermes faced him. There was a sour look on his
face this time. He stuck out his tongue and shuddered
once.

"What now?" whispered Apollo.

"She's kissing him," Hermes whispered back, "and
with her tongue too."

Apollo went into spasms of revulsion followed by
a shudder. He led their retreat outside.

Hermes followed Apollo all the way to the gate.
"I knew I should've brought the camcorder."

At their own broken gate, Apollo veered off down
the sidewalk. "I'll be right back. Try to stay out of
trouble while I'm gone. That means: Don't wander off."

"Wander off? And miss seeing the look on Mars'
face when he finally comes outside? You couldn't drag
me from this spot." Leaning on the gateposts, Hermes
turned to watch Udela's bedroom window where it faced

the street. From his vantage point he could see not only her bedroom window, but also the back door. He said to himself, "Mars really does have a strong stomach."

Apollo ambled back with a grocery bag dangling from his left arm and a cardboard tray bearing three grande-sized espressos balanced in his hands. "Espresso?" he said.

"Don't mind if I do." Hermes took one.

Apollo glanced at his wristwatch. "He hasn't come outside yet?"

Hermes shrugged.

The back door opened. Mars stepped outside and sedately closed the back door without so much as a hair out of place. There was however a somber look of mortification on his otherwise stoical features as he joined his comrades. He met their glances and after a long moment, said, "I feel so dirty."

Apollo held out the tray. "I got your favorite. I figured that you'd need a boost after your ordeal."

Mars took the cup that Apollo angled toward him, saying, "You are a god. I worship at your feet."

Apollo bowed slightly. "I thank you."

They let Mars take a long restorative drink of his espresso, watched him close his eyes in gratitude, and open them with a little of his better humor again.

"What's in the shopping bag, Apollo?" Mars said.

"The biggest bottle of rubbing alcohol I could find and a big, fat sponge. I figured that you'd want to sterilize yourself afterwards."

Mars gave him a fierce embrace. "I love you, man."

As he stepped back, Apollo handed over the bag. "Get thee hence and purify thyself."

"Gladly." Mars moved past them toward their

own back door, but paused. "What are you grinning at, you pervert?"

"How was it?" said Hermes.

Apollo made a face. "Hermes."

"You know you're curious too. Come on, Mars. Talk."

"A gentleman doesn't kiss and tell."

"A gentleman wouldn't, but the God of War would. Spill it," Hermes commanded him.

Mars eyed her bedroom window. "Her reputation is well-warranted. And she's mighty well preserved for a 56 year old. Not bad at all." He strolled toward their back door.

"Really?" said Hermes.

Mars stopped and turned. The smile he wore was wicked. "You don't believe me? Well, you will soon enough." He chuckled.

Hermes' smile vanished. "Why? What did you do? You said something. What did you say?"

"We just had ourselves a lovely little pillow talk. I confided my concerns to her about my younger brother."

Apollo drank his coffee like a good boy and stayed well out of it.

"What did you say to her?" said Hermes.

"I confided to her that my poor brother had absolutely no luck in love."

"You didn't!"

Mars nodded. "I chalked it up to a lack of confidence. She promises to be gentle with you, but a word of advice, 'little brother', when she gets her hands on you, just do whatever she wants." Swinging the grocery bag, Mars chuckled all the way inside.

Hermes dropped his espresso and didn't even notice that he had.

8. Aiken's Amorous Aura

It all started with a pack of fags, not that there hadn't been a few odd incidents en route to stir up his already queasy nerves, but stepping into the newsagents' on the corner to get some cigs was when it became glaringly apparent that something had changed.

He asked for his favorite brand and received it, not only readily and with a most fetching smile from a girl normally too bored to look him in the face, but gratis too. The girl flirted with him the entire time, smiling, speaking lowly so that he had to lean in close to hear her, which had the added benefit of allowing him a generous look down her cleavage, and caressed his hand as she handed him his pack of cigarettes. She told him when she had lunch and where she'd be having it and how close that was to her flat. She repeated this bit of beguiling information three times. Aiken teased her by saying he'd think about it, if he could squeeze it in his schedule, but they both knew he'd turn up.

As he turned away to leave, Aiken was feeling mighty pleased with himself. What in the world did he have to be nervous about? Then he saw arrayed between himself and freedom several other women, including the girl's mother and grandmother, neither of whom had ever given him so much as a cross-eyed glance before. All stood before him gazing with glassy, bedazzled expressions, smiling, as immovable as slumbering cows.

He faltered. That nervous feeling grabbed his

stomach and SQUEEZED, but then he realized that it wasn't entirely in his imagination. A rather determined, bony hand stroked his left butt cheek and then pinched it even as he lurched aside. The girl's Gran winked at him.

Aiken sped away from there. Only after he'd crossed the street he looked back and saw them all still gathered watching him with fierce, feverish eyes and unnatural, unchanging smiles. They looked like zombies stoned out on pot.

Aiken fled.

At first he was too distracted to notice, but increasingly he kept having to sidestep women. He thought nothing of it other than that the sidewalks were unusually crowded even for a Saturday morning. The more he stepped aside though the more they seemed to block his way. Their hands reached out and caught at his arms as they peered up into his face. They all had the same bright, glistening feverish look in their eyes. All spoke in bedroom voices and smiled with feline intent. A few were even bolder with their sinuously stroking fingers. He flinched and hopped violently each time, looking rather like a disjointed marionette.

Soon his path stood clogged with them and Aiken was forced to a stand still. Then they all pressed in.

How he broke clear he couldn't quite say, but one moment he stood trapped among a small, but swelling sea of smiling, staring women, and the next he was sprinting madly down the center of the lane dodging cars and lorries. His freedom had cost him his leather jacket. He glanced back. The women warred over it, shredding it. Those who could not get close enough to grab at it turned to gaze after Aiken. Where their gazes turned so did their feet.

Aiken ran harder than he ever had in his entire life.

Three whole blocks blurred past before he realized that it might have been better if he had been running toward home and not even further away from it. Breathless, he stopped and looked back.

All the women he had rushed past had stopped and now stood gazing after him, falling under his spell. Even as he watched, their eyes took on that terrible, feverish gleam of desire. Then one by one they turned his way.

AIKEN RAN.

Veering around a corner, he spied an alley and ducked down it. A door opened just ahead and a burly man came out with two sacks of rubbish.

"Stevens!"

Stevens stubbled face broke into a great round smile. "Aiken! Is Haley after you again? I thought you'd paid him back." This last he shouted after Aiken as he ran past Stevens into his pub.

"Hurry! Shut the bloody door before they see," Aiken hissed back.

Stevens grinned even wider and shaking his head, tossed the rubbish in the bin. "They? What sort of trouble are you in now?"

"Just come in and shut the door."

Frowning only slightly, Stevens closed the door and ambled behind the counter. It occurred to Aiken that he had never seen his friend move faster than a purposeful stroll or look anything worse than stern and that was in a crisis, a rare occurrence actually. "Coffee?" Stevens said.

Aiken nodded as he subdued his wild breathing and tilted his ear toward the front door. He made certain to stand at the far end of the bar where he wouldn't be visible from the front windows. Shadows began to pass the windowpanes. He ducked down behind the bar. "Don't look at me. I'm not here."

Stevens frowned at the windows way over on the other side of pub. A mob of women, some of them regulars and neighbors, passed the windows. Several stopped and, cupping their hands beside their faces, peered in. He stared back at them as he poured a cup of coffee.

Light refracted brightly again into the pub. Stevens handed the cup down to Aiken. "What did you do, mate?"

"Shagged the wrong bird." Aiken raised the cup to his lips, but stopped. "Where's the wife?"

"In Spain, still." Stevens sighed. "Here I was thinking I'd be reveling in an artificial bachelorhood – dishes in the sink, running about the house in me knickers, and what happens? I miss the wife. 'Wouldn't dare make a mess that she'd have to clean up, so I've been a right good boy the whole time. The house is spotless." Stevens sighed again and took a long meditative sip from his own cup.

"Do you mind if I hole up here for awhile?"

"Stay as long as you like – or as long as you need to." Stevens winked at him.

Aiken sighed and drank his coffee. That's when he noticed that his own hands were trembling.

When opening time approached, Aiken hid in the back office. Stevens didn't look too surprised .He grinned and shook his head.

"Don't tell anyone I'm here or that you even saw me," Aiken added as he closed the door.

That seemed to amuse Stevens even more, but he nodded, saying, "Not a word, mate."

Aiken locked himself in and settled behind the desk with the telly on, but turned down to a whisper. It was going to be a long day.

In the front room, Stevens leaned against his bar and wondered why the women wandered back and forth in front of his pub. Now and then, one would peer in, but not seeing anything other than big burly Stevens and his steaming cup of coffee, resumed restlessly wandering to and fro looking all about. He frowned and that frown deepened a little more as time passed. When he finally opened the front door, he knew they would come inside and something told him that they wouldn't go away easily.

9. Mid-Day Saturday: Marshall's Wrecking Crew

Her amorous morning romp lay well and truly in the past. In fact, it might as well have never happened judging by Marshall's imperturbable matter of fact attitude when he set to work on her house. In response to her most inviting smile, her new lover had given her only a look of calm, smiling calm, unperturbed and yet analytical calm, and shouldered past her with his equipment.

Then she had met Hermes' glance and saw a shock of panic strobe through his light eyes and remembered. He looked like quite a healthy colt, and although she would have liked another ride on that athletic stallion Marshall, he had suggested she give Hermes the benefit of her expertise. As though reading her thoughts, the young man scampered inside past her, reeking of fear.

And then all hell broke loose.

With a swing of Marshall's sledgehammer, the renovations began with gusto and there was nothing to do but flee outside.

Udela paced and alternately pressed her hands to her face or clenched them together in anguish. Alarming sounds came from her home. Hammers, saws, and drills created a discordant concerto of sorts. The neighbors had complained several times already, but there was no stopping the wrecking crew she had unleashed upon her neat, perfect home. Every time she spied a neighbor staring her way, she pretended to fuss over her roses until they lost interest.

She was adjusting her immaculate lawn furniture yet again when, behind her, Medusa and Athena came outside. They settled around the red picnic table, and scratched at the dried paint on their hands and arms.

Athena pointed. "You've got a speck on your nose, Medusa."

Medusa crossed her eyes to look at it and letting go a small sound of exasperation, rubbed it off. Then she looked across the way and, smiling at the racket coming from next door, called out, "Mrs. Dunk, how are the renovations coming along?"

Udela rushed to the fence. "Do they know what they're doing?"

Athena grinned crookedly. "Indeed, Mrs. Dunk, they know PRECISELY what they're doing."

"They're experienced then?"

"No, but they're fast learners," said Medusa.

As though they had heard this disquieting statement, which they probably did, a great, horrible bang erupted from the Dunk house that made the whole place shiver and shed dust.

Hermes' voice piped up from the ruined house's depths. "Oops! Sorry."

With his arms shielding his head, Erian burst outside. In his wake, a series of deadly thuds resounded.

Udela caught him in her arms. "What's happening?"

He cast wild eyes back at the house. "The floor will be on the ceiling and the ceiling on the floor before they're done."

"But I gave them only the simplest list of projects."

"Mum, I've seen the list. For all intents and

purposes, you've asked them for a whole new house."

"Ask and ye shall receive," said Athena.

Erian frowned at her.

Athena narrowed her eyes right back.

Erian shifted – just enough to keep his formidable mother between himself and his nemesis.

"Well, at least they haven't broken anything yet," said Udela.

Just then, right on cue naturally, something shattered. Dead silence fell over the Dunk household.

"Spoke too soon," said Medusa.

Udela's hands flew to her heart. "Tell me that wasn't - "

Beaming, Mars poked his head outside. "I'm sorry, Mrs. Dunk, but you know that lovely punch bowl - "

"But it was Eighteenth Century!"

"Was it? Oh. Well. Don't worry. We'll find you a replacement at a car boot sale." Mars ducked back inside.

Udela sat down hard. Erian got too close. She seized his arm.

"Ow! Mum!"

"Go inside and keep them away from the china cabinet. If my china – "

An ominous groaning sound issued forth from within, followed by what could best be described as an horrific, god-awful, crash.

"My china! Oh! Go in! Go in!" She shoved her middle son toward the back door.

Erian stumbled inside. Silence settled over the Dunk household as heavily as a deep dark thundercloud over a sunny meadow.

Udela wrung her hands.

"You get what you paid for," commented Athena.

"But I haven't paid – "

"My point exactly."

Erian came back outside. For a moment he glanced longingly toward the gate and avoided meeting his mother's gaze.

"Well?" said Udela.

Erian's mouth went dry.

Mars poked his head outside again, just as sunny as he could be. "Uh. Mrs. Dunk, we had a little mishap with your cabinet, but we'll hammer it back together again."

"But my china?"

"Don't worry. I'll buy you some paper plates - the good kind, not the cheap ones."

"You've broken my best things! I've a good mind not to reimburse you at all."

Mars' grin broadened. "Whatever you say." He ducked back inside.

One pregnant pause later, Apollo and Hermes hooted and cackled and then the pounding and thumping resumed in earnest.

Udela raked her hands through her hair. "What have I done?"

Medusa grinned and shook her head. "I'm going in for some punch, Athena. Want some?"

"Sure. Anything to wash the taste of paint out of my mouth."

Medusa slouched inside.

Erian eyed Athena. Athena was pretending to be engrossed with her fingernails. He wasn't fooled. "Mum, there's something I have to tell you," he said lowly.

"What?" she grumbled.

"Our neighbors...They're different from us."

"They're hippies. You said so yourself."

"No. No. I was wrong. They're something else..."

Athena smiled over at him.

"Something worse, Mum."

"You aren't saying that they belong to a cult, are you?" Udela gazed at her back door, thinking with fresh, but reluctant distaste of her interlude with Marshall. He couldn't be in a cult. He was too keen-eyed and sharp-witted for that.

Erian drew her further aside. He failed to notice the lessening, more idle noises coming from his home or that Hermes looked out past the curtains at them. "No, Mum. Their names – that was the clue. Minerva is another name given to Athena the Goddess of Wisdom. Phoebus is another name for Apollo. Venus IS Venus or Aphrodite. Marshall – well, obviously, he's Mars, or rather, Ares. Medusa is obvious too, and Herman, that wing logo on his cap is a dead giveaway that he's really Hermes, the messenger to the Gods."

So that was it. Udela gave him a long hard look, one that threatened to turn into disinterest. "And you know this how?"

"I have proof! About Athena at least."

Udela sighed. "Let's see it then."

"It's in my room."

Hermes withdrew from sight.

"Go and get it," she said.

"Yes, Mum."

The racket inside resumed an idle bumping as Erian crept inside.

Athena approached the fence. "Ahem."

Udela looked her way.

Athena motioned to her. "Do you mind if I ask you a question, Mrs. Dunk?"

"What is it?"

"It is of a personal nature." Since Udela stood immovable with her arms folded across her breast, Athena felt obliged to add, "I'm concerned you see."

"What is YOUR dilemma?"

Athena's brow arched. "It isn't me I'm concerned about."

At last, a look of interest flitted across Udela's face. "Oh?"

"It's your son Erian."

She narrowed her eyes. "What business is he of yours?"

"Well, it is a delicate matter, so I wasn't certain whether it was my place to bring it up."

"Go on."

"Has Erian been under some peculiar strain recently?"

"What makes you think he has?" she snapped.

"If he hasn't, then I'd hesitate to diagnose him."

Udela began to grow exasperated. "Diagnose him for what?"

"Has he been under stress recently?"

"I couldn't say. When he is at home, he lays about the house all day with his nose buried in his books, or barricaded in his room with his computer, looking at porn most likely."

Apollo sauntered out with one hand behind his back.

Athena stroked her chin dramatically. "Hmmmm," she went.

"Are you a psychiatrist?" said Udela.

Athena gestured at Apollo. "No, but Phoebus is

an expert in the medical field, and I do believe that he has been observing Erian's behaviour out of habit, right, Phoebus?"

Udela lunged toward Apollo. "Do you think something is amiss with my son?"

Only briefly startled, he side-stepped her, and eased up alongside Athena's spot beside the fence. "Which one?" Apollo leaned against the fence and very casually let his right arm drape down on Athena's side. In his hand, he shook Erian's 'proof'.

Athena snatched it all and hid it behind her back. "Erian of course!"

Apollo circled his finger beside his head and whistled. "Sorry, dear. He's blown a fuse." He shrugged. "I mean, seriously, he thinks I AM the Greek God Apollo."

"And what are you?"

"A hippie." With that, Apollo gave her a taut grin that was not at all friendly, and headed back through her backdoor just as Erian returned outside wearing a confounded look on his face.

Erian quickly took on a narrow-lidded glare as Apollo passed him wearing a most guileless and boyish grin. The instant Apollo had closed the Dunks' back door behind him the symphony of thumps, thuds, slams, and bangs, stopped short. Erian cast a wary look at Athena and motioned to his mother.

"What is it?" she said.

"Come here."

Barely masking her annoyance, his mother drew nearer.

Erian leaned in close. "I can't find them."

"Find what?"

"The proof!" He quickly lowered his voice again.

"The proof. I had printed up all these articles and photos off of the internet and now I can't find them."

"Print more then."

"That's just it, Mum."

Athena aimed an innocent smile in his direction.

"I can't even find the information on the internet anymore. It's as though someone…"

Hermes chose that moment to venture outside and stretch.

" – Erased it."

Hermes winked at him just as another unfortunate crash, a dull plastic one – came from the house. There were further plastic crashes down the stairs.

Apollo poked his head outside. "Ohhh. I'm sorry, Erian, but… " and he held out the printer's wretched remains by its electrical cord, "…I dropped a hammer on your nice color printer, accidentally."

"But of course," snapped Erian.

"And that sound was your computer bouncing downstairs," said Hermes. "Oops. Butterfingers."

Erian's jaw dropped.

Apollo jogged Hermes in the arm. "Come on. There's still work to be done."

"Coming, Phoebus."

As soon as they had gone back inside, Erian caught his mother's arm. "It's all a plot, Mum. That was the real Hermes and the real Apollo – just as that is the real Athena over there smirking at me."

"Of course they are." Udela patted his cheek and tilted her head sideways, peering into his eyes. So much for his being the brightest of her brood.

"Don't look at me that way. I'm not daft, Mum. I'll prove it. I'll get the proof."

"You do that. Look, there's Mrs. Nesbit with her

darling new kitten." Giving her middle child a sorry look, Udela headed for her gate and, passed in front of her house, heading for Mrs. Nesbit's next door.

As soon as she passed from sight, Athena whistled at Erian and waved the pilfered proof at him. The tongue she stuck out at him only added insult to the injury.

Erian rushed at the fence. "What do you want with us?"

Athena drew out each word. "Don't - you – wish – you - knew?"

Stewart strolled into sight. In the midst of all the chaos and noise swirling about his home, he saw and heard only his Juliet where she nestled against him matching his distracted stride.

Erian spied him only shortly before Athena did. "Mum's been looking for you."

"No, she hasn't," said Stewart. Juliet faltered, but Stewart squeezed her shoulders as they drew up to the gate.

Udela backed away from her neighbor's front yard. "Yes, it is interesting how that kitten shows up the very morning that your old cat disappears. 'Must go now. That racket? I've got men in renovating today. Yes! I can't wait till they've finished either."

The smile Udela wore for Mrs. Nesbit's benefit fell away the instant she returned to her own gate. At least the sounds erupting from her home had grown sparse and sporadic, but who knew how long that lull would last? Then she saw Juliet sheltering in Stewart's embrace and a morning crammed to overflowing with aggravations found a welcome outlet.

"I should have known. This explains everything. Have you come to finish off Stewart?"

"No. I came to get him out of here," said Juliet.

Udela approached her in the manner a fox approached the hen house. "And what does your husband think of that?"

Not in the least bit cowed, Juliet retorted, "If my 'ex' was sober enough to have even one coherent thought about it, it still wouldn't make any difference where I'm concerned."

"So you've finally made up your mind that it's my Stewart you want."

"Stewart was the only one I ever wanted."

Udela's expression turned smug and plainly mean. "Aiken will be interested to hear that."

"What does Aiken have to do with this?" said Stewart.

"Why don't you ask dear sweet Juliet here?" said Udela.

"What does she mean?" said Stewart.

Juliet shook her head and with more fury than grief, wiped the tears from her eyes.

Udela gloated at her discomfort. "Ask Aiken yourself, if she won't tell you the truth. After all, look how readily she bounced from you to your brother to Roddy – and now back to dear, dependable Stewart."

Stewart gripped Juliet's hand firmly in his own. "Yes, I am so very dependable. Where would you be, if you didn't have me around to abuse on that score?"

Quick to smell an impending assault upon her authority, Udela bristled. "What was that supposed to mean?"

Medusa came outside with two glasses of punch. Athena pressed her finger to her lips and motioned for her to sit down beside her. Instead, Medusa sat at the far end and scooting Athena's glass to her, mouthed, "What is it?"

Athena jerked her thumb over her shoulder.

"Leave Juliet alone," Stewart was saying.

Udela turned cold and concise. "What did you MEAN by that last remark?"

"Meaning that, IF you depended on just Aiken or Erian to provide for you, your clothing would be your advertising and you'd have a legitimate excuse to be out all night every night."

Medusa and Athena exchanged looks and mouthed simultaneously, 'Oh my God!'

Erian and Juliet gulped.

"How dare you after all…?"

"…After all, I'm not the only one who noticed that I'm the only one who actually looks like my Pop."

Even the racket inside the Dunk house had stopped altogether. Mars and Apollo peeked out the windows with their mouths hanging open. Poking his head through the doorway, Hermes wore an eager grin. As soon as she pivoted their way, they ducked out of sight.

Udela huffed and puffed and marched inside. Her refuge was brief. A cry went up and out she rushed. She stumbled into Erian's embrace. He guided her toward one of her immaculate lawn chairs, where she sat with her hands pressed to her bosom.

Finally she caught her breath. "My house! What have they done to my house?"

"They said that they were doing only what was on your list," said Erian.

"They've wrecked the whole bloody house!"

As sharp as lightning, Mars' voice cracked forth from within. "Up. Up. To the left. My left. And… "

Wham!

"What was that?!" said Erian. "An anvil?"

Again Mars' voice resounded forth from within. "No. It's off center. Up. Up. My right – just a smidgen more and - "

Wham! The Dunk household turned to gelatin and quivered dangerously.

"Go in! Go in!" cried Udela. "Stop them!"

Even Stewart was impressed to see how bravely Erian charged back inside.

"One more time," shouted Mars. "Up! Up! Easy and – now!"

Whump! Crash!

"Bulls eye!" Mars shouted triumphantly.

Erian came back outside, saw his mother and tried to veer out the gate.

Udela lunged out for him. "That wasn't the antique mantelpiece?"

Erian rubbed his arm and sprung just out of her reach. "Noooo. Actually it was the couch."

"Not the chintz?"

"That's the one you won't let us sit upon, right?"

Udela nodded.

"You don't have to worry about anyone sitting on it anymore."

"Why is that?"

"Because they flattened it…"

Udela gasped.

"…With the mantelpiece."

Udela flung herself to her feet, arms flailing. "They must be stopped."

She ran inside – and shrieked.

In the midst of all the chaos, Athena, joined swiftly by Venus, motioned at Stewart and Juliet to come into their yard.

"You'd best hide over here until it all blows over," said Athena.

The instant Stewart and Juliet set foot through the gaping gate, Venus hurried the couple into their house. "Stay in here until the coast is clear."

Udela's voice shook the windows nearly out of their panes. "Out! Out! The lot of you! OUT! You've made a wreck of everything! GET OUT!"

Grinning and ducking, they shielded their heads with their arms. Hermes led the retreat out of the Dunk household. Less fearful, Mars strolled out last and stopped on the patio with his arms raised out imploringly from his sides. Udela appeared in the doorway armed with a broom.

"But, Udela, the job is only half finished," said Mars.

"If I don't stop you now, I won't have a house left to live in."

"I'll tell you what. We'll take a break, have luncheon, and then come back and fix it all."

From her threshold, Udela shook her broom at him. "You'll do nothing of the sort. Stay out of my house. And don't you dare address me as Udela ever again."

"Very well." Mars turned away, smiling hugely.

Udela slammed the door.

Already, Hermes had re-gained the sanctuary of their back yard wasteland.

Apollo lingered within their gaping gate for Mars to catch up. "Does this mean we're done?"

"Nope," said Mars. "As soon as the devastation soaks in, she'll be begging us to finish and we'll be ready." He chuckled and rubbed his hands together. "Come on. I'll show you what I've got in mind."

They headed for the back door. Hermes tried to skulk around them toward the sidewalk.

"No, you don't. Inside with you." Apollo caught him about the neck and propelled him inside the back door first.

"No running off until we've finished," said Mars.

Athena locked eyes with Erian and kept smiling at him until he fled out onto the sidewalk.

"Where is Aiken anyway?" Erian groused.

Erian sped down the sidewalk, risking only the briefest of glances back at Athena, who gave him a little wave. As soon as he was gone, Athena sat on the edge of the picnic table and began skimming through Erian's proof with an amused expression on her face.

Stewart and Juliet peeked through the open back door and crept out.

Medusa jogged Stewart on the arm as she headed back inside. "You stood up to your mother. Good for you. In honor of your bravery, I'm going to bake some biscuits."

"That's lovely," said Venus, "but we mustn't eat too many. I'm working on a savory halibut stew."

Their reaction was striking. Medusa stumbled on the last step and had to catch herself from falling. The papers in Athena's hands tumbled upon the grass, but Athena herself sat frozen. Horror lit up sizzling hell fires of dread in her formerly serene eyes. Although it took a moment, Medusa recovered and trod the rest of the way inside.

Athena stayed put, but as Venus herded Stewart and Juliet over to the picnic table, she put on her best poker face.

"If you don't mind my asking, Juliet," said Venus, "what does Udela have against you? You seem perfectly sweet to me."

"Yeah, what happened?" said Athena after she had recovered some use of her wits. She stooped over and picked up the papers and also the discs that had fallen.

"What makes you think anything happened?" said Juliet.

Venus and Athena exchanged looks.

Venus draped an arm about Juliet's shoulders. "Perhaps we should talk alone with Juliet for a few moments."

"Stewart, I think you need to go inside," said Athena.

"No, I don't think so."

Athena's tone was only slightly sharper than her glance. "Yes, you do. Go inside. NOW."

"Yes, and keep the lads out of Medusa's hair while she makes her goodies," said Venus.

Stewart sighed. "All right."

"Good boy. But if our boys tick her off and you see her reach for that red bandana," began Venus.

"Cover your eyes – FAST," said Athena.

Stewart's pace toward their back door faltered. After a moment, he said, "All right."

As though expecting an ambush, he crept inside. A great shout went up and for an instant they saw Stewart's flailing arms and one foot in the doorway. Then he was gone.

"Whoops," said Athena. "Apollo must need a guinea pig for one of his experiments."

Juliet took half a step after him. "Guinea pig?"

Athena shrugged. "Whatever. He'll be fine."

Venus sat Juliet beside Athena. "I sense that something happened or you would have never left Stewart."

Juliet wrung her hands and fidgeted. She looked at Athena.

Her tone was stern, but Athena returned her gaze with eyes full of compassion. "It involved Aiken, didn't it?"

Juliet smiled, but she had to wipe sudden tears from her face. "This stays between us?"

"Of course," said Athena.

Juliet looked up at Venus.

"I would only tell Medusa." Venus sat on Juliet's other side and rested her arm about her shoulders. "We're in this together."

Juliet nodded and wiped her face again. "I've never been able to discuss this with anyone. Stew and I had been sweethearts since we were sixteen. We had been talking about getting married. He was the only man I saw myself ever marrying."

"Why do I get the feeling that Udela didn't approve?" said Venus.

"She couldn't tolerate even the sight of me and she was always trying to steer Stewart away from me. Aiken was worse."

Athena's gaze turned piercing. "What did he do?"

Juliet shuddered and seemed to fold into herself. The two Goddesses exchanged looks.

"When Stewart wasn't around, Aiken was after me constantly. He would say lewd things to me. He was always promising to show me what he could do."

"And then?" said Venus.

"One night he did." Juliet flung herself to her feet and paced, tugging at her fingers all the while. "It was my own bloody fault. Stewart and I had been celebrating. He had just been hired for the job that got him where he is now. He had asked me to elope with him that weekend before his job started. We came back here so he could pack, but Udela was having one of her hypochondriac spells, so he had to go off on some daft errand. I waited for him out here – just over there behind the shrubs and the garden shed. I remember being so afraid that something would go wrong."

"Here. Stop a minute before you start hyperventilating." Athena stood and reached out to stay her for a moment.

"I'm fine. Really." Juliet tried to smile, but it was a grimace. " 'Best to get this over with, right?"

Both Goddesses gazed back with somber expressions.

"Aiken found me. Like I said, Stewart and I had been celebrating down at the pub. He must have seen us there or someone must have told him, because I remember Stewart telling someone there about our plan. They bought us a round to wish us good luck. – It seemed like forever, but not five minutes after Stewart left, Aiken came right to me."

Venus caught her hand and peered up into her face. "He didn't?"

The manner in which Juliet buried her face in her hands was answer enough.

"That bastard son of a bitch," snarled Athena.

In an instant, Venus had taken Juliet into her arms and rocked her until her emotions calmed. "So you left because of Aiken."

Once the gate had finally been opened, the truth could only gush out. "Udela came outside looking for Aiken. He said he'd tell Stewart. I was too upset. I told Udela."

Athena leaned toward her. "You told Udela what Aiken had done?"

Juliet nodded.

Exchanging stark looks with Venus, Athena said, "Did she believe you?"

"She saw me. She saw what he had done – and she didn't care. I should have stayed. I should have stood my ground."

"You should have gone to the police," said Athena.

"Who would they have believed? Udela would have covered for her precious Aiken."

"Well, we believe you," said Venus.

Athena frowned at the ground. "So Udela knew all along."

Juliet nodded and wiped away her tears.

"Then why did you get married to that other guy?" said Venus.

Juliet's face flushed. "Panic. Anger. Despair. Bloody–minded stupidity. Aiken kept telling me what he'd say to Stewart about our little liaison. Udela just stood there smiling at me, puffing away like a chimney on her fags. I couldn't bear the thought of facing Stewart then. What if he didn't believe me? What if he hated me?"

"Here. Sit down and calm yourself." This time, Venus would not be refused.

Once again Juliet found herself book-ended by the two Goddesses, allies for the time being.

"As you must be aware by now," said Athena, "they didn't tell Stewart anything – for the very simple reason that they knew that Stewart would get angry enough to do something about it."

"You must tell Stewart the truth," said Venus.

"I can't. I just can't."

"You must. Otherwise it'll fester in the back of

Stewart's mind," said Athena. "Your flight felt like an absolute repudiation to him – an abandonment."

"Tell him," said Venus.

"What about Aiken?" said Juliet with a wild glance.

Sharing the same inspiration, Athena and Venus exchanged smart little wolverine smiles.

"It's too cruel," said Venus.

"But it's so appropriate, and besides, when we tell her, who'll be able to stop her?" said Athena.

"We'll take care of Aiken," said Venus. "Never fear, Juliet."

"Where is God's gift to women anyway, Aphrodite?" said Athena.

"Becoming acquainted with the true meaning –and consequences - of that phrase."

Athena's eyes lit up. "What did you do to him?"

"He thinks he's irresistible to women and now he truly is."

Although Juliet couldn't help, but smile at how heartily Athena chortled and slapped her knee, she gave the two women an odd, wondering look.

At that instant, almost unrecognizable from the mauling he'd received, Aiken came tearing back. His clothing, what survived of it, had been reduced to ragged streamers. He slammed past his own gate, and with great desperate, weary strides, ran into his home. A great rattling crash followed the sound of the back door's slam.

Udela shrieked, "Aiken!"

Aiken shouted, "You didn't see me. You didn't see me!"

Erian stalked back. His gaze tracked along behind a relentless thought scuttling home on the sidewalk ahead of him. At the Dunks' gate though, his gaze fell upon Venus and Athena where they still sat beside Juliet. His step faltered.

Just as sweet as she could be, Venus smiled and batted her eyelashes. The only thing missing, aside from the little harp-strumming cherubim floating about her lovely, shining presence, was the halo of pseudo-innocence. She came forward as far as the fence and leaned upon it.

Erian pointed a stern finger at her. "You're responsible for this."

"Responsible for what?"

"Every woman on the block is panting at the sight of him and the men want to beat him to a pulp. Admit it. You're responsible."

"I'll admit it right enough, but I doubt that it'll make you feel any better or give Aiken a reprieve. Payback's a bitch and so am I when the mood strikes me."

"That's it. I've got it now." Erian snapped his fingers. "You're in league with the Prince of Darkness."

"I've never heard Hades called that before," muttered Athena.

Venus smiled alluringly. "Now that I've done for Aiken, is there anything and I mean, ANYTHING I can do for you?"

Erian's accusatory finger dropped to his side. His mouth went small and all living color drained from his face. Then a flash of inspiration struck. "I'll find a priest. He'll exorcise the lot of you." Off he sped.

Athena snorted. "I would love to be the fly on that priest's wall: 'Father Mulligan, Venus the Goddess of Love put a hex on my brother. Ares, Apollo, and Hermes are renovating me Mum's house, and the Goddess of Wisdom is out to get me.' The look that will be on his face…"

Juliet eyed both women in their mirth. It occurred to her that Stewart's description of his new neighbors as being 'different' was putting it a little too mildly. There was something quicksilver about them that she glimpsed in their glances and that seemed to shimmer just beneath their mortal skins. Stewart had also said that these strangers had been determined to befriend him and looked 'daggers' at his brothers Aiken and Erian, whenever they came around. That had been good enough to win her favor. The question had to be asked though. "Who are you people?"

Still smiling, the two women exchanged looks.

"It's a good thing you're sitting down," said Athena.

10. The Unpleasant Truths of a Late Saturday Afternoon

Stewart and Juliet sat huddled together at the far end of the picnic table that was set anew with bowls and spoons. The disturbing sight of Athena and Medusa sitting midway down the table with horror frozen in their stares had them wondering whether they shouldn't clear off. Medusa kept rocking and muttering to herself.

"If Athena doesn't stop biting her nails, she won't have any nails left," whispered Juliet.

"Athena? Ow," hissed Stewart. "You pinched my hand again."

"Sorry."

"Honestly. What's wrong?"

"Everything's fine."

"Are you sure? Ever since this afternoon you've been preoccupied. Something is upsetting you." Stewart made her look him in the face.

"You've been preoccupied too, and I think it's my fault."

Stewart looked down the table at his odd new neighbors and their very odd behaviour. "I wouldn't be so sure about that."

Juliet sighed. "There's something I need to tell you."

Stewart felt his stomach twist in a knot. He had never liked that particular tone of voice, especially with those sorts of phrases. It usually meant pure bad news or something so overwhelmingly unpleasant that his sun would be blotted out for a while. "About what?"

"I need to tell you why I left."

He felt as though sharp fingernails stood poised above old tender scars. Soon he would bleed as vigorously as a hemophiliac. "There's nothing to explain anymore. You've come back."

"But there is."

"No. No. It's fine really." Waving his hands close to his ears, Stewart stood up and began pacing.

Athena and Medusa watched him, their own anxieties forgotten for the moment.

In an instant Juliet had leapt after him and seized his hands, which she stroked as much to calm her nerves as his. She tried to look up into his eyes, but he averted his face. "I didn't leave because of you."

Stewart stopped utterly still. After a long moment, he looked into her eyes with a gaze as clear and fragile as glass.

Juliet met Athena's glance and then followed it to Medusa, only to see her amber eyes take on a frightening glow. She shuddered at the Gorgon's potent glance. At once, she grasped Stewart by the arm and led him through the gaping gate. "I need to talk to you alone."

Athena watched until the couple walked out of her sight, then she studied her nails and made tsk-tsk sounds.

As insouciant as ever, Hermes bounded through the gaping gate with a smile for all present Shirking off work early always put him in a sunny mood. " 'Evening all. What's for supper?"

"Halibut soup. Poseidon's recipe…supposedly," said Athena.

"Oh?"

Medusa gave him a meaningful look. "Venus is cooking it."

If Hermes had stopped any more abruptly, he would have given himself whiplash. "She must be stopped." Veering hard to the right, Hermes had not taken two steps toward the back door when Mars and Apollo trudged outside.

"Too late," grumbled Mars.

Hermes pivoted toward the gate. "I'm not hungry."

Apollo and Mars snagged him and steered him firmly toward the picnic table. Hermes dragged his feet every step of the way.

"If we have to suffer, so do you," said Apollo.

With heavy sighs, the three Gods took their places at the picnic table. Hermes broke free and assumed Stewart's former place – as far as he could go without Mars having to tackle him to keep him there. At any rate, he figured he had a clear shot through the gate just in case there were hors d'oeuvres.

There the five sat behind those wide, deep bowls and grappled with their emotions.

"I'm scared," said Medusa.

"Me too," said Mars.

Beaming, Venus sallied forth from the kitchen. From her right hand hung a great, fat witch's kettle from which a great ponderous sloshing could be heard.

"It's going to turn us into slugs. I just know it," muttered Athena.

Apollo leaned toward Mars and said lowly, "It would help if we knew what the ingredients were."

"Love? Darling?" called Mars.

"Yes, sweetie?"

They watched her set the kettle dead center upon the table. Curiously, neither steam nor any aroma crept out from beneath the lid, except for a subtle briny, salty seawater smell.

"What's in this recipe?" said Mars.

"Halibut," said Venus.

"But what else?" said Mars. "Garlic? Onion? Pepper?"

"Just halibut. What else would there be in halibut stew? Oh! I forgot the ladle. I'll be right back."

They waited until the back screen door bounced shut behind her then they shot to their feet and watched.

"Here goes nothing." Bracing himself, Apollo touched the lid and found it cool to the touch. "Oh. Hmmm..." He took a deep breath and raised the lid.

"Is that what I think it is?" said Athena.

"It's a tuna fish," said Mars. "Two of them."

Medusa snorted. "Tuna? She couldn't even get THAT right."

"They're live too." Apollo took on a crooked grin and scratched his head.

"Runty little things, aren't they? Are you sure they aren't guppies?" said Hermes.

Naturally, both tuna fish took offense and, splashing as they adjusted positions, they then...

"Now that's just plain rude!" said Medusa.

"Wow. I didn't know that a fish could flip the bird," said Apollo. "Now I've seen everything."

"Cover them. Close the lid, Apollo." Athena plopped down on the bench again. "We can't eat this."

"It could have been worse," said Hermes.

"How so?" said Athena.

"She might have used piranha."

Looks of horror passed between them all.

"Who wants pizza?" Mars whipped out his cell phone as he sat down again.

Four deities thrust their hands into the air.

"You know, Aphrodite's a heavenly girl, and I love her dearly, but she can't butter toast to save the world." Mars nodded at them. "Hello? Hello. Two large pizzas if you please – one loaded with pepperoni and a vegetarian special. Yes? Perfect. No. We'll send someone 'round. Thank you." He flicked the phone shut and his wallet open. He tossed a five-pound note at Apollo. "If everyone will contribute, Hermes will get the pizzas."

Apollo added his share, then Athena and Medusa, and finally Hermes as he received the money.

"Hermes, see if you can't speed things along," said Mars. "I'm starving."

"I'll just pop into the time stream and pop right back."

"Oh, and one more thing." Mars lifted the kettle up by its handle and with his lip curled up in disgust held it out toward Hermes. "While you're en route, be so good as to liberate our dinner guests."

"Right."

Whistling the whole way, Hermes departed with pizza money in one hand and the kettle with the irate tuna fish in the other.

Juliet's hand trembled in his. Stewart's heart pounded. She rushed him to the far corner and stopped hard and suddenly. Breathlessly, she looked all about and clung tight to his hand. "Let's see if I can get through this," she muttered as she faced him.

Stewart grabbed the bull by the horns. "You said that you didn't leave because of me."

"I didn't."

"Why then?" His stomach quivered. He felt as though he would be sick, that, or as though the earth was about to swallow him up. He didn't know which would be worse.

"Do you remember that night? That night we were going to elope?"

"How could I forget?"

Her words began to rush. He didn't interrupt her, but her grip on his hand tightened even as it shook.

"I hid where you left me behind the shed. I became drowsy…"

"Well, we'd had a bit much to drink," Stewart said.

Juliet shook her head. "I should have really fought back. I didn't fight hard enough. I should have bit and clawed."

A hard cold anger shot through Stewart. "What happened?" His voice burned low, level, and hard.

"Aiken. Not five minutes after you left, I think. It was sudden. I wasn't prepared, but then how could anyone be prepared under the circumstances, right? I remember thinking that you had come back." Juliet shoved away the tears with her hands and fought them back with her frown. She saw Stewart's eyes squeeze shut and watched him avert his face. He knew, but her words fell as hard as stones. "He grabbed me. He… I couldn't. I tried, but not hard enough. He ra…"

Stewart laid his fingers over her lips. "Why didn't…?"

"Your mother."

He blinked and tilted his head. "My Mother?"

"She knew."

Stewart staggered back. They let go of each other's hand. "You could have told me."

"No. I didn't think I could. She would've sided with your brother against me and said that I threw myself at him."

"Do you honestly think that I would ever take their word over yours, Juliet?"

"I...I was so scared," she said, but it was as though a great shaft of light cut through the center of her being.

"You were the only one I ever believed in."

Juliet let go a sob. "I'm so sorry. I'm sorry." And yet the pain she had carried about for so long began to ebb.

"YOU have nothing to apologize for," he said in a tone she had never heard before.

He turned and marched. His stride turned brisk, furious.

Stewart charged past Hermes going the other way. Juliet tried to catch him but he was past his gate and inside his house before she could stop him. She dared go no further than the Dunk's fence.

Juliet turned toward Athena. "He's furious. I don't know what he's going to do."

A series of crashes rumbled from within the Dunk household.

Udela began shouting, "Stewart! Stop it. Stop it."

Aiken stumbled outside. Driven from his last refuge, he looked about, but saw no way to escape. His whole world had gone to hell in the space of a day and decided to take him along whether he liked it or not.

Stewart ripped through the back door. Only his mother's arms wrapped about him kept him from setting upon his eldest brother in absolute fury. "I know what you did to Juliet. Bastard!"

"What are you talking about?" said Aiken.

"Think back to a night in this very garden. Mum sent me on one of her bloody stupid errands and I had left Juliet waiting for me. She ran away after that night."

A slow, ugly smile rose upon Aiken's face. "Sure. I remember. I remember how she threw herself at me."

"That's a lie!" Juliet shouted.

Aiken flinched. He hadn't seen her standing off to the side.

Udela released Stewart and interposed herself quickly between him and her favorite. "Just like she threw herself at Roddy. She married him fast enough, didn't she? And not a word from her since, until suddenly she shows up wanting to make amends and all. She didn't tell you that her husband's business had failed and that he was on the dole, did she?"

Stewart gazed past Udela to Juliet. "Is that much true?"

Juliet stood with her fierce gaze leveled upon Udela. "That was nearly two years ago, and it failed because he preferred being inside a pub more than being inside his office. He lost our lease - everything."

"She took her sweet time coming back," sneered Aiken.

Juliet struggled for words. "I wasn't well."

Udela smirked and nodded her head. "That's putting it lightly. She was in a mental hospital."

Juliet stared at her a moment. Had Udela been keeping tabs on her all this time? "I'll tell you this much, Udela, IF I'd heard that someone had dropped a house on you and Aiken, I'd have come back in a heartbeat."

"Where she was doesn't matter. She's here now and we're leaving together. And, you," and Stewart pointed at Aiken, "you'd better stay out of my sight from now on. Juliet, I've got some things to pack. I'll meet you at your house in an hour."

Giving Udela one last seething look, Juliet marched off with her arms clasped about herself.

Stewart glared at his mother and brother, daring them to say even one more word, to dare lay so much as a finger on him for so much as an instant. Neither of them made a move, except for Udela putting a protective arm about Aiken. Stewart slammed the back door behind him.

Udela tried to examine Aiken's nose.

Aiken shrugged her off. "Leave me be." Not thinking, he went off down the sidewalk.

Udela watched him go, but when her attention reverted to her own home, her anxious expression hardened. She was not done yet, so in she went. "It's a good thing you are leaving, Stewart. It saves me the trouble of throwing you out!"

Another door slammed, Stewart's bedroom door most likely.

Medusa's eyes were narrowed. The Date Rape Avenger had 'arrived'. "What exactly did Aiken do to Juliet?"

"I'll tell you later," said Athena.

"Why not now?"

"I'd rather wait until the time is more opportune, if you get my drift."

Medusa cocked her brow and took on a sly smile. "You have a plot in mind."

"I do, so bear with me."

"I'll endeavor to be patient." Medusa cast a gleaming look of vicious longing at Aiken's receding back.

Hermes zipped back, pizza boxes in hand. Mars rushed to the gate to relieve him of the top box. Venus re-emerged with ladle in hand. Both Mars and Hermes froze.

Venus stopped at the picnic table and frowned

most prettily. "Where's my halibut stew? Mars?" She turned. Her jaw dropped. "Pizza? Where did the pizza come from? And where is my halibut stew?"

Before them stretched a minefield. They approached it with great care while their minds darted hither and yon for some convincing explanation, or excuse, or both.

"The pizza fairy!" said Hermes as though it were a perfectly natural explanation. He shrugged with well-practiced nonchalance.

Venus wasn't buying it. "The pizza fairy?" Certainly the arch that kinked her brow was an ill omen.

"Yeah, the pizza fairy loves halibut stew." Hermes leaned close to Mars. "Right, Mars?"

"Leave me out of this." Mars took both pizza boxes, but not before Hermes snagged a piece of the pepperoni pizza.

"Does he really?" Venus propped her hands on her hips and cocked her head.

Hermes scampered after Mars and sat at his usual end of the table atop the barrel where he proceeded to wolf down his first slice and then a second.

Apollo, Athena and Medusa were already elbowing each other to get their share.

Mars held out a vegetable laden slice to Venus. "Sit down and have a slice."

For an answer, Venus folded her arms across her breast and glared at Mars.

"Suit yourself." Mars dropped the slice back in the box and after slapping Hermes' hand aside, pried out two slices of pepperoni pizza.

"What happened to my halibut stew?" said Venus.

Looks were exchanged.

Hermes shrugged. She'd have to be able to catch

him before she could enact any horrible punishment upon him. "Firstly, THEY were tuna fish, and secondly, I liberated them." He made a swimming motion with his free hand.

"You returned them to the ocean?" she cried.

Mars shrugged. "Your stew was a noble effort though, love."

"Aphrodite, Dear," said Medusa as kindly as she could, "face the facts. The only thing you're any good at is meddling in people's love lives."

Athena snorted, "That's debatable."

"And what was that supposed to mean?" Venus' glare shifted to Athena, much to Mars' relief.

Athena fixed her calm, fearless gaze upon her. "Like Medusa said, you really aren't that good at much of anything else, except meddling in people's lives. Frankly, your cooking is the scariest thing this side of Hades."

"I haven't exactly had a lot of practice," said Venus.

"No kidding," said Hermes.

"But with a little more practice …"

"Oh no! No. No," said Athena. "You are not using us as guinea pigs anymore."

"But I've got steak tartar and crab salad planned for tonight."

An angry bellow emerged from the work shed beside the house. Two long horns rammed through the broken slats along the top of the door and shook it nearly off of its hinges.

Apollo turned as pale as the moon. "Dear Lord, no."

They envisioned a live bull, unskinned, all red and dripping with barbeque hot sauce, and none too happy about it either. In particular Hermes saw himself having to be the one to rope the damn thing, wash it, and some-how drag it into the kitchen without being gutted by its horns. As for the crab salad, - well, they saw the bed of lettuce artfully arranged in a bowl and clustered at its center they saw six crabs snapping their claws at them every time they came too close. It would be a dish with 'bite'. Bellowing again, the bull withdrew its horns and stomped about within the shed, snorting and smashing things.

Athena shot to her feet. "I call a vote! Those in favor of banning Venus from the kitchen forever after — raise your hands!"

Five arms shot into the air.

"This isn't fair," cried Venus.

"Five yeas and one abstention," said Athena.

"Wait a minute!"

"The vote is carried. The proposal has been passed. You are henceforth banned from the kitchen. That means: no more cooking, ever."

"What do you have against me, Athena?"

"Aside from your atrocious cooking?"

Apollo gave Athena a warning look.

Athena disregarded it.

"I really want to know, Athena. You are always belittling my gifts, insulting my intelligence…."

As surely as though they'd caught a whiff of electricity in the evening air presaging a massive storm, Hermes and Medusa exchanged looks and, taking a piece of pizza each, moved a little further up the yard. There they stood, eating and watching the situation exacerbate with expressions just a little too bright with eagerness. This confrontation had been brewing since the days of a certain conflict in the Aegean.

"…Ever since Troy as a matter of fact," concluded Venus.

"Bulls eye!" said Athena.

"This is going to be good," said Hermes.

Medusa shushed him so she wouldn't miss a word.

"Ladies," said Apollo, "that was a very long time ago. Water under the bridge."

"Come on. Have some pizza, love." Mars even held out another piece to her.

Venus slapped it out of his hand without removing her gaze from Athena's glare.

"Okay," said Mars. He and Apollo backed away a safe distance, just far enough not to get caught in the crossfire, but not so far that they couldn't leap into the fray, if things turned truly ugly.

Venus smirked. "You're still sore that Paris didn't pick you."

"You cheated," retorted Athena.

"I WAS the most beautiful. And as I recall, I wasn't the only one bribing him."

"I offered him a life choice."

"So did I."

"An intangible."

"And true love isn't?"

"You offered him another man's wife."

"It was destiny."

"It was a bloody kidnapping."

"They coupled eagerly enough alone that first night."

"Are you kidding? Alone in a camp surrounded by her kidnapper's men? Eager, my ass! Helen was terrified for her life. Of course she submitted to Paris."

"Theirs was a great and passionate love. It has been sung of down through the centuries."

"If it was so damn passionate, how come they never had any children? Huh??? Explain that to me:

how a couple could be together for ten years without so much as a miscarriage? Hmmmm? Nothing?"

Venus stood her ground, eyes blazing, arms folded firm across her breast.

Athena ventured nearer, step by step. "I'll tell you why – "

"I knew you would. You do love the sound of your own voice."

"Ah – Ah. I won't be sidetracked – not this time. Love was the last thing in Paris' mind. You knew that the line of succession, the very right of rule, passed through the female line. Whoever possessed Helen, possessed the right to rule Sparta in Menelaus' place. You not only caused an innocent woman to be abducted and raped, you attempted to overthrow the rightful King of Sparta, who actually did love Helen."

"Paris earned the right to possess Helen's passion."

"Some passion! Interesting how quickly, how readily, Helen returned home with Menelaus. Helen was a prisoner of Troy and nothing more."

"I did what I had to in the name of love."

Athena was beside herself. "You caused a horrible war! All those lives were lost because you had to have that stupid golden apple."

"I am the Goddess of Love and Beauty. I deserved it!"

"You're spoiled and selfish, and you're more trouble than you're worth."

Mars and Apollo stepped between them at once.

"Uh, Athena," said Apollo, smiling nervously. "Perhaps you're being just a little harsh. This is all in the past, remember?"

Athena shook with anger. "What she did was

wrong."

Apollo kept his voice calm. "It may have been."

"It was, Apollo," Athena insisted.

"All the same, it is in the past. If you will remember, Troy was my city, under my specific protection and patronage…"

"You didn't start the whole mess."

"No, but I did kill your cherished hero Achilles, and you haven't held that against me. Let it go."

Venus leaned around Mars. "Yes, you forgave Apollo. You can be cordial even with Mars here, but you can't treat me with common decent respect."

"I will when you merit it," snapped Athena.

"You pathetic, sour old Vestal. This isn't over."

"I'm shaking." Athena mock-quailed, then straightened up again. "Do your worst. I'm immune to you."

Venus' eyes narrowed into gleaming slits. "We'll see about that."

Stepping aside from Apollo, Athena strode past Venus toward their back door. Neither Goddess risked so much as a glance away from the other. They snarled at one another, "Bitch!"

Athena stomped inside and slammed the door behind her.

Hermes snapped his fingers. "Damn. I was hoping for a catfight."

Medusa sighed. "It's early yet."

Hermes nudged her. "Let's go watch Aiken fend off the women."

Medusa cackled fiendishly. "Let's!"

As giddy as puppies fresh from their naps, the pair charged down the sidewalk.

Wearing an expression bed-rocked with granite,

Udela came back outside. She shut her back door with particular emphasis behind her. The clearing sound she made in her throat was redundant.

Mars muttered, "Uh oh."

Apollo pivoted.

"There you are." Udela stood nodding angrily.

"And where else would we be?" said Apollo.

"None of your games. I don't know what you've done or what you're up to, but I'll thank you for staying out of my family's affairs."

Mars smirked. "What makes you think we've done anything?"

"Until you moved in, everything was fine, but now Erian makes no sense, Aiken is terrified of women, and my lovely home is an absolute wreck."

"You'll notice," said Apollo lowly, "that she didn't mention Stewart."

"If you'd let us finish, your house won't be a wreck anymore – that we CAN fix," said Mars as pleasantly as he could manage, which was hard since he was enjoying her predicament so damn much.

Udela pointed her finger at him. "No more nonsense? And you'll fix what you smashed?"

Both Mars and Apollo held up their hands.

"Scout's honor, ma'am," said Mars.

"Let's get our gear," said Apollo.

"No!" Udela held her hands up. "Tomorrow morning."

"Are you sure?" said Apollo, innocently.

"Yes, my nerves are in such a state."

"Same time tomorrow then?" said Mars with a look at Apollo.

Apollo sighed and nodded like one anticipating a root canal.

Udela hesitated as she turned toward her back door. "Yes," she said after a moment's thought. Her stare remained fixed upon the too bright smile that Mars kept focused on her. She thoroughly regretted ever getting close to him.

As soon as she had shut her back door behind her, Mars slapped Apollo on the shoulder.

Apollo's brow arched. "You've something special in mind, don't you?"

"Fresh inspiration." Rubbing his hands together, Mars chortled as he headed inside.

Apollo chuckled and turned again to eye the Dunk household. He kept expecting to see Stewart charging out with his belongings shoved in his backpack. Then he felt it, the stark sensation of two eyes boring white-hot holes deep into his back. The feeling was relentless, irresistible – he had to look.

Venus smiled.

Apollo knew that look. "OH NO."

Venus sat to the picnic table and up popped her little sign: THE DOCTOR IS "IN".

Backing away, Apollo shook his hands at her. "No. Please. No."

Venus gestured to the opposing bench. "I said we'd have ourselves a little talk one day."

Apollo backed two more steps toward the gaping gate. "No. Really. This isn't necessary."

"Have a seat."

"Please – "

"SIT."

Apollo slumped and hung his head – and did as she commanded. He plopped down hard and folded his arms brusquely over his chest. "There. Happy now?"

"Ecstatic, sweetie. Now, about your love life…"

Apollo cringed and longingly looked past her at the gaping gate.

"Don't even think of scampering. I'll sic Eros onto you. Now, I've been considering your situation. You have a serious problem."

"No, I don't. Everything's fine."

"All evidence to the contrary..."

Apollo stared at the ground and kicked at a tuft of grass.

"Let's run through some names, shall we?" said Venus.

"Let's not."

"Cassandra of Troy. What happened there?"

"She rejected me."

"Louder please. That almighty noise you boys made this morning at the Dunk house sabotaged my hearing."

"I offered her the gift of prescience in exchange for her sexual favors."

"Remind me. How did that turn out?"

"She agreed to sleep with me so I gave her the ability to foretell the future."

"And then?"

Apollo glared at her. "She reneged on the deal, so I cursed her: She'd still be able to tell the future but no one would believe her."

"And thereby you helped to doom your own city: Troy."

Apollo twisted his mouth, grimacing. "All right. All right."

"Daphne."

Apollo banged his head on the picnic table and left it resting there. "She ran away from me."

"And?"

"Then she turned into a tree."

Venus shook her head and made disapproving noises. "Just to get away from you."

Apollo raised his head and turned his back on her. With particular emphasis, he refolded his arms over his chest. " 'Finished yet?"

"Not by a long shot. Let's see. There's Dryope, Marpessa, …"

"Do you have a point? If so, I would appreciate it if you would get to it and stop rubbing salt in my wounds."

"Actually, I do have a point."

Apollo braced himself. "Let's hear it."

"I think the real reason that none of your previous amours worked out is because quite simply you hadn't directed your energies toward the one person who truly suited you."

Apollo remained dubious. "Uh – huh."

"Someone very close to you."

Apollo stared back. His eyes narrowed. He waited for another clue to drop from her infernally smiling lips.

"Someone who is your true other half."

"Not Artemis?!" Apollo halfway bolted up from his seat.

"No, not her!"

"Whew!" He settled down again. "You scared me for a minute." The shudder that followed came naturally.

"Did you really think I'd suggest her? Give me a little credit."

"Who did you have in mind, Venus?"

"This is the best possible person for you. You would make a truly golden couple."

"Fine. Who is it?"

"As it was, both of you were second only to Zeus in our little pantheon."

"Who is it?"

"When I tell you, it will seem so stunningly obvious."

"As obvious as the pimple on your nose?"

Her hand shot to her nose. "I do not have a pimple!"

"You will in a minute, if you don't get on with it."

"You can be so impatient."

"Venus!"

"And that's why all of your courtships have been such disasters."

"Do you have any lemon to go with the salt you're rubbing in my wounds?"

"This time if you handle the situation right, you'll have your heart's desire at long last."

"That's all very well, but you still haven't told me who Miss Right is."

"It's Athena."

Apollo began to snort, but stopped. Realization genuinely dawned across the sun god's face. Actually, it flashed across his face like a super nova and left quite an afterglow.

Venus peered round for a look at the expression on his face and smiled. "There! That did it."

Athena darted out the back door, but Mars' hand in her hair stopped her escape. "Ow! Ow! Ow."

Mars thrust his other hand outside. From it hung a very large, pendulous plastic bag. "It's your turn to put out the rubbish."

"Bully." Athena accepted it. The second rubbish bag bounced off her face and landed on her feet. "Pig."

Mars chortled as he withdrew.

Venus watched how Apollo's gaze followed Athena as she slumped and bumped out through the gate, slung the bags into place beside the sidewalk, and turned back. She leaned close to whisper into his ear. "Remember, a little patience this time."

Apollo nodded and muttered something.

In her opinion, dreamy incoherence was a good sign. The bright, sharp-toothed smile of an incorrigible vixen lit up Venus' face as she patted him on the shoulder and fairly strutted toward the house. "You know, this is a truly lovely evening. Why don't you take a break, Athena?"

Athena stopped and cocked her head at her. "It's my turn to wash the dishes or what's left of them."

"I'll do that, dearest."

"Dearest? But there's the laundry to do too."

"Consider it done. Oh, and Hermes is going to Firenze for gelato later."

"Does he know he's doing this?" said Athena.

"No, but he's about to find out."

Athena didn't catch the thumbs up sign Venus gave Apollo. Instead, she shuffled toward him, paused to stretch, and then sat down near Apollo, who leaned attentively toward her. She eyed their back door a moment. "I think she's up to something."

"She has a good idea now and then."

Athena gave him a long look. The look she received in return brimmed almost to overflowing with admiration and adoration, quite a tender look actually, and almost certainly one she wasn't accustomed to receiving from anyone. Confusion flushed across her face before concern lowered her brow. "Are you feeling quite all right?" she said.

"I am feeling the entire universe at this moment —

from the greatest nebula to the smallest particle."

"You'll need an aspirin then." Athena began to move.

Apollo seized her hand to stay her and admired it with lingering caresses. "No. I'm fine for once."

Athena yanked her hand free. "All right! Where did he shoot you?"

A quick check of his head ensued. Athena's fingers raced through his lustrous fiery hair in search of that telltale wound. She did not notice how Apollo took on a serene smile, closed his eyes, and finally sighed. He re-opened them when she began poking and prodding and tapping at his torso and arms in quest of that dreaded wound. Of course there was none, for Venus' words had proven just as effective as poison and left just as minute a trace as well. Judging by Apollo's beaming countenance, he was suffering no ill effects whatsoever.

Athena struggled with a billowing sense of alarm. "All right, I saw you out here at this table with that meddler. What did she do?"

Apollo's gaze traveled all across her face. "All this time you've been right under my nose."

"I'm going to kill her."

Apollo seized both of her hands. "No. You mustn't. Can't you see? She has done us both a great favor."

For a moment, Athena was too stunned to react. "Which is?"

"Pointing out the obvious: We two make the absolutely perfect match." Excited by his comprehension of it all, Apollo released her hands and began pacing about the table. He smacked his hands together and held them so. "We are the two well-balanced halves of one perfect whole."

"Don't go all Pythagorean on me. I'm not in the mood." Up she stood and with one purpose in mind: to throttle Venus. Or at least give her a sound thrashing with her own gilded sandals.

However, Apollo was at her side in an instant and seized hold of her right hand. She pried her hand loose, so he grabbed her left hand.

"Hey!" She pulled that hand loose.

He caught the other one with a growing grin.

"Stop that!"

This time he caught both of her hands and held them fast as he leaned toward her.

Athena leaned away. "What are you doing?"

"What do you think?"

Athena fell backward, but his grip on her hands broke her fall. She landed with a mild, if undignified whump. The startled look on Athena's face caused Apollo to break out laughing.

Bewildered and piqued all at one, Athena yanked her hands free and had just sprung to her feet when Mars darted outside.

In his rude chef's apron, Mars stood with his right arm pointing back into the house. "Athena! You have to stop her."

Athena resumed standing. "Venus again." She leveled a clear, calm gaze at Apollo, whose disturbingly beatific smile had returned. "What is she doing now?"

"She's trying to wash the clothes and dishes simultaneously. She's stuffing the saucers in with the socks as we speak."

"Has she any sense at all?" Athena charged inside.

In mere seconds, Venus appeared outside the back door as though run outside by an ax-wielding lunatic. She quickly concealed her look of flustered discomfiture with a smile that she aimed at Mars. With a kiss for his strong chin, Venus propelled Mars back inside with the mildest of touches.

As soon as Mars was within, her attention reverted to Apollo. "Broken the ice yet?"

"I've made a preliminary overture."

"You didn't get carried away?"

"I was the epitome of courtly restraint."

"You must be, or Athena would be halfway to Alaska by now – with you in hot pursuit, no doubt."

Apollo grinned and nodded. "You live, you learn."

"Very good. Now, you must court her."

"Court her?"

"Oh, that's right. Your idea of courtship is to see someone, conceive a great passion, and light out after them in the manner of a starving cheetah after a gazelle."

"Hey!"

"Ah – Ah! No arguments. You need to make a traditional gesture. Something that shows you have manners and are not an overheated octopus."

"But I'm a sun god. I can't help the heat."

The Dunks' back door opened. Udela barged outside.

Stewart glowered resentfully in her wake. "I say we should leave them both where they are for their own good."

Venus patted Apollo on the shoulder. "Go consult the Muses, Apollo. Go on. Don't worry. I'll look after everything."

"Right." Hands shoved in his pockets, Apollo's head bent forward as couplets formed in his mind already. He strolled through the gaping gate and off down the sidewalk.

Venus leaned upon the fence wearing a sweet neighborly expression. "Is something amiss?"

Stewart opened his mouth, but Udela was the one who spoke in tones all a quiver with violent emotion.

"This is all your doing – the lot of you. I believe I asked you malcontents, you pagans, to stay away."

"I'm sorry," Venus smiled and batted her eyelashes, "but today was my house cleaning day, so I haven't a clue what you're talking about."

Stewart took on a lopsided grin. Luckily his Mum hadn't sprouted eyes in the back of her head yet.

Udela's fury darkened her face and narrowed her eyes. She stalked around the corner of the house, muttering, "Whore of Babylon."

Stewart lingered behind though.

Venus groused, "Whore of Babylon indeed! Just wait 'til I tell Inanna. What happened, Stewart? Why haven't you fled?'"

"I didn't run away fast enough." Stewart sighed. "Actually there is a crisis."

"Aiken and Erian, right?"

Stewart grinned and pointed at his nose.

Venus grinned. "What happened?"

"It seems that Erian went off to find an exorcist, but he frightened the priest so badly that the police had to be called."

"And Aiken?"

"A mob of women chased him straight up a tree. The police AND the fire department had to be called to rescue him. Right now he sits in the same cell as Erian. They're both in police custody for their own protection."

"Poor Aiken. All those women."

"And men too. Apparently there were a good number of angry husbands and boyfriends waiting for

Aiken to come down out of that treetop. Isn't it marvel-
ous?"

"Something tells me that he'll be a different man
from now on."

Stewart gave her a reappraising look. "Why do I
have the horrible feeling that you had something to do
with that?"

"Because you know I did."

Udela shouted from their driveway, "Stewart!"

Stewart backed toward his gate. "Mum is off to
bail them out and I have to drive. If Juliet comes looking
for me, tell her what happened and that I'll be back when
this mess has been cleared up."

He shrugged and trooped off to join her by the
family car. He pulled out in no great haste while his
mother ranted about their infernal neighbors.

Hermes bounced though the gaping gate, whistling.

Venus pointed a finger at him, stopping him in
mid-bounce. "Firenze. Now. Gelato."

The whistling stopped. His smile turned into a
scowl. Hermes pivoted and stomped back off, casting a
mutinous look back as he went.

Venus walked forward as far as the gaping gate
and watched to make certain that he went in the right direction. "I saw that look. Hey! I saw that too. You're
going to get it! Mars! Hermes needs another thrashing."

Mars' weary voice came out through the kitchen
window. "What did he do now?"

Venus stomped inside.

For a moment all was stillness and tranquility. In
the gathering twilight, the nightingale sung its little aria
uninterrupted for a change. Something in the kitchen
crashed. Athena ducked outside and closed the door on

the smashing and shouting going on between Mars and Medusa. Neither was happy unless they were picking on the other.

Medusa's voice rose up loud, "I'll turn them loose, and when I do, it's the sculpture garden for you, smart ass."

From Athena's hand hung another rubbish bag stuffed perilously full. She didn't even bother marching all the way out through the gate to place this bag with the rest. Instead, she walked up to the fence and flung the bag over the side. Sighing, she turned away and stretched. Yes, it was turning into a fine, mild evening.

Apollo popped up on the other side of the fence, his gleaming eyes riveted upon Athena.

Athena stopped. She frowned. Apollo ducked. She looked back. Nothing there. That didn't ease her nerves. The very air about her seemed to simmer with energy.

It had been a long day and felt longer. She shuffled toward the picnic table. Perhaps she'd stretch out on top of it and stare at some old associates in the night sky. A groan escaped Athena as she eased herself onto the bench and settled back into a prone position.

Rather than the first stars of the night blinking forth from the deepening blue velvet sky, Athena found herself looking directly up into Apollo's face. She flinched and covered her face with her arms. "Oh! Don't do that!"

"I'm sorry. I didn't mean to startle you," he purred. "I've written a little poem. Would you like to hear it?"

Athena sat up and mulled it over a moment. It occurred to her that dogs sitting at their masters' feet under the supper table wore similar expressions of barely contained impatience. "You'll read it whether I say yea or nay, won't you?"

Apollo's grin widened as he bobbed his tousled head.

"Let's hear it then."

The haste with which Apollo sat beside her and drew out a sheaf of papers disconcerted Athena almost as much as the ponderous width of the epic itself.

"Ready?" he said.

Athena gave him a dubious look, complete with arched brow and narrowed eyes.

Nothing deflated Apollo's infernally sunny mood though. He cleared his throat. "I call it 'Ever Near' or 'Ode to She of the Flashing Eyes'. I wrote it myself."

Athena shook her head and rolled her eyes toward the heavens in hopes that a lightening bolt might deliver her. The skies remained sparkling and clear. There was nothing she could do but humor him. His poem would probably take some time, so she leaned upon her knees and hung her head.

Apollo began,
" 'How many, how often have voices beseeching
Unto mine ears been raised
In their innocence or despair seeking
An answer to this simple prayer
For a life their heart deserved?' "

"Shakespeare was busy, eh?" said Athena.
"He was hung over. Quiet now."

" 'How often have I heard their cries
And heeded them in their sufferings
While alone crossed I their azure skies
Illuminating alike lives humble and exalted

Without any hope of ease for my own longings?' "

"Keats was busy too, eh?"
"Too ill. Shhh."

" 'My mind thus resigned now dawned a fateful day.
Three simple words in kindness spoken
And suddenly ahead a new path before me lay.
Saith she who knoweth best:
I know whom you seek, your heart need no longer beat broken.' "

"This does have a point, right?"
"PATIENCE, Athena."

" 'Ever near' with her flashing eyes
Clever, unsleeping, motherless child' "

"I do too have a mother or did until Zeus ate her."
Apollo stole an irritated glance at Athena as he went on…

" 'Hath the grey-eyed goddess for ages stood nigh:
Champion of humanity,
Prometheus' consolation,
Destroyer, commander, wise, serene and maidenly mild' "

Athena's head shot up and she narrowed her eyes at him.

" 'Let my prayer join with the rest
If I too should attain

A life my heart desires best:
Bring me good luck and happiness.
My joy my poor heart can no longer contain.' "

"Let me see that." Athena reached for the poem.
Apollo held it just out of her reach.

" 'The truth and she who embodies it embraced at
last
And let Mount Olympus with our joyous nuptials
sing.' "
"Let me have it, Apollo."
"'Two souls perfectly united –' "
"Give it to me, Apollo."
"Hey! Let go of it."
"Let me have it."
"I'm still reading it."
"I can read it for myself."
"I wrote it for you, Athena."
"Then let me read it."
"You're going to tear it!"
"Then let go of it."
"You're spoiling everything."
Athena got a good secure grip on one end of the
manuscript and with the other began to rap on his hands.
"Let go. Let go. Let go."
"Ow. Ow. Ow. Ow!" He let go.
"Thank you very much." Angling herself so that
she faced away from Apollo, his wounded looks and his
hand flailing, Athena frowned over the poem.
Perhaps it was just as well that she was reading it
for herself. His bright expression returned. He shifted
close beside her so he could peer over her shoulder. She
shot a scowl at him. He shifted a few inches away and

examined the little red welts where she had smacked his hands. As soon as she resumed reading, he shifted nearer and peered over her shoulder again. Her eyes widened. Then her jaw began to drop as she devoured page after page covered with his elegant, archaic manuscript.

" 'You like it?" he said.

"Heavens!"

"I knew you'd like it. Wait until you get to the section about our honeymoon. The words just flowed from my pen."

Aghast, Athena skimmed through the details of their 'impending' wedding and the celestial celebrations that would attend that. When she stopped flipping rapidly through the pages, he knew she'd found it.

"Gracious!"

"I was truly inspired when I wrote that: Our wedding night."

"Golden thighs…lingam…yoni…nectar…virgin sacrifice!"

"I consulted the Kama Sutra for that passage actually."

"Oh my God!"

"Oh, you found the illustrations! Gustav Klimt was nice enough to do them for me."

"And in color too. Would you look at that? Ummm. Lovely."

In an instant, Athena stood and thrust the stack of papers back into Apollo's hands. Startled, he nearly dropped them all over the lawn instead.

"All right. This has been diverting." Athena moved several feet away from him.

"You didn't like it?" His expression was as vulnerable as a little boy's, which disconcerted Athena.

Choosing her words carefully, Athena said, "It was

an honorable effort."

"Tell me you thought it at least a little diverting."

"Yes, but not as diverting as what I'm about to do to Venus." She headed for the back door. The fists she held clenched at her sides she raised only to pound together, one into the palm of the other.

Apollo stood up. "Athena!"

Athena stopped just outside of their back door. Her hand gripped the door handle. "What?"

"You didn't give me your answer."

"Answer?"

Apollo waved the pages at her. "To this! It's a proposal of marriage. You didn't give me your reply."

Athena felt her courage seep out through her toes. Be evasive. Yes! That would work. Be evasive. "Reply to what?" Or she could just pretend to be a dimwit.

Apollo didn't fall for it. "To a very simple question. Will you marry me?"

His simple directness made her pause. "Oh. Ah. Let me think about it. First I have to throttle someone."

Apollo flinched at the door's slam and watched for a moment, expecting the whole house to explode. Instead, silence fell over the yard and not the peaceful all-is-fine kind of silence either. Even the birds went mute and waited to see what might be coming.

He heard Hermes before he saw him. The Rossini melody he whistled flitted upon the evening breezes, a feather could not have drifted with such easy grace as Hermes' melody. Two clear shopping bags swung from his hands as with a leap and a spring Hermes landed within the gaping gate.

With a flourish Hermes raised the bags, but the smile on his face vanished. "Gela – . Something's wrong. I can feel it." Wild of eye, he spun about as though he expected a tiger to come leaping out of the shrubbery. "Apollo?" he called without risking a look at him. "Something's wrong? What is it?"

"Athena is going to kill Aphrodite," said Apollo glumly.

"Is that all?" Shaking his head, Hermes joined Apollo.

"She's in a real state this time." He brooded over his poem.

"So what else is new? Be honest. It doesn't take much to get either of them in a state."

Apollo grunted.

"Why are you so glum?"

"Poetry."

"Dude, you really should steer clear of Edgar Allan Poe."

Apollo rolled his eyes.

The back door flew open so violently that it broke on its hinges. Venus ran out with Athena close behind with her sharp angry fingers stretched out after the Goddess of Love.

Venus ran one way around the picnic table. "How's it going?"

Apollo shouted after her. "Terrible. She hates my poem."

Athena glared at her from the other end. Her famous grey eyes flashed ominously. She lunged to one side and Venus ducked the other.

Venus made a run toward the gaping gate, but Athena blocked her escape so that she had to run to the far side of the picnic table. "Are you sure? I think you hit a nerve."

Athena lunged for her. Venus yelped and just escaped her clutches. Hermes clutched the gelato-laden shopping bags close and hunkered down. The Goddesses exchanged positions. The breathless stand off continued.

"You think so?" Apollo's gaze settled in bright hope upon Athena again.

Venus nodded. "Keep it up. You're making progress."

"But what if she turns into a tree?"

Venus snorted.

Athena let go a cry of absolute fury and flew around the table after her. Both blurred into the house just past Medusa, who glanced with a bored expression after them.

Medusa's expression lit up when she saw the shopping bags Hermes held. "There you are! Bring the gelato in before it melts."

"Huh – uh! I'm not getting caught in that crossfire."

Medusa peered in through the open back door. "No, it's under control now. Mars is holding them apart. You can come in.

"I think I'll wait."

Medusa grabbed him and propelled him shopping bags and all toward the back door. "You big baby. You know that if things get out of hand, I'll just unleash the lads. A little enforced stillness might bring them to their senses."

Apollo had to smile at that. The smile triggered a notion or two, and out through the gate he darted. He returned to the gate just in time to witness Mars wrestling Athena outside and then shoving her toward the gate.

"Take a walk. Thanks to you we don't get to have gelato tonight. You need to calm down." Mars pointed out at the greater world beyond their fence.

"She didn't?" said Apollo.

"She did – dumped it all over Venus," said Mars. " 'Fairly plastered her with gelato."

Apollo shook his head and made disapproving sounds.

"When she can apologize she can come back inside – and not before." To make certain of it, Mars folded his arms across his chest and stood guard on that very spot.

Athena was in a self-righteous huff. "Fine. I'm going for a walk."

"Good. Why don't you get lost while you're at it," said Mars.

"You wish, Ares."

Athena raised her chin, straightened her clothes with several fierce tugs, and turning onto the gate path, nearly walked into Apollo. His gaze was warm and appraising, his smile quiet and decidedly intimate.

"What now?" said Athena.

Apollo reached behind his back and whipped out

...

"Roses?" she said.

- Which he thrust into her hands.

"No!" She flung them to the side as though they were poison ivy branches.

Not believing what he was seeing, Mars had to move closer.

Apollo then produced an open box of –

"Chocolate?" she cried.

- And popped one into her startled mouth before she could even gasp. Athena spat it out. Apollo gave her a quick smooch. She swung. He ducked. Mars was a little slow though. He fell back against the fence with his hand pressed to his face. Athena just began to stammer out an apology when Apollo seized her hand, and with a speed and grace that dazzled, slid a ring onto her finger and kissed it.

Even Mars gawked at this development from where he sat on the grass.

The sound that escaped Athena was somewhere between a howl, a shriek, and an agonized moan. It would have taken two dogs, a fishwife, and a banshee to duplicate her cry of outrage and horror. Coherent speech returned, but no matter how furiously she pulled and clawed… "No. Oh NO."

The ring wouldn't come off.

"Oh YES! Superglue!" said Apollo. "That baby ain't comin' off for nobody."

Mars leapt to his feet and clasped their hands together. "To quote your good buddy Shakespeare – 'Tis a match'." Enjoying her dismay, he slapped Athena on the shoulder. "Congratulations, Sis."

Delighted beyond any previous experience, Apollo planted a kiss on Athena. She slapped him. Mars burst out laughing. She swung at him. He ducked. Apollo chuckled. She stomped on his foot. Apollo hopped up and down. Another gale of laughter burst out of Mars. Athena lunged at him, but he fled inside and held the door shut so that she wouldn't get to him.

No amount of shoving, pounding and kicking could budge Mars. Even though his chortling needled her so badly that it provoked a real tantrum, he remained braced against the door and she blocked out. Finally, Athena had to stop and catch her breath. She leaned upon the door and glanced out upon their humdrum neighborhood.

"Has the world gone utterly mad?" she said toward the sky above them.

Neither the moon, nor the stars, nor anyone dwelling amongst them offered her a reply. She sighed and brushed some loose strands of hair from her face. The unfamiliar new sparkle coming from her ring finger stopped her. Another sound of aggravation escaped her. She tugged again.

"It will never come off," said Apollo.

Athena shook her hand at him. "This can't be happening. I'm Athena, damn it."

Step by careful step, Apollo approached with his hands clasped behind his back lest he spook his willful bride. "I am well aware of that."

Athena looked up. Her gaze was sharp. "I'll cut this hand off if that's what it takes."

He caught her hand and stroked it. "And spoil your lovely arms? You mustn't even think of such sacrilege."

"Then remove this from my finger."

"Never." Apollo clasped her hand to his heart.

"Stop that."

Apollo smiled. "No."

"Let go."

"Make me."

Athena shrugged. "Very well." She stomped first on one foot. Then the other. Naturally, he let go.

If she had hoped to infuriate him, she failed utterly, judging by his grin and the kindling light glowing from his eyes. That, and the fact that he recovered from the stomping in mere seconds, and rested his hand upon the fence as he leaned toward her.

There was nothing to do, but make a run for it, which she realized – a split second after diving through the gaping gate toward the open street – was the absolute worst thing she could have done. There are some critters you just shouldn't run away from: lions, tigers, grizzly bears, rabid wolverines, and Apollo! Unfortunately, once you started running from Apollo, your options became extremely limited. Either you escaped his hot-blooded embrace by turning into a tree or some other inanimate object, or you let him catch you and you dealt with him and the consequences.

Now, there was no way Athena would resort to sprouting green shoots or blooms, and the alternative seemed unthinkable, but even that possibility seemed less and less improbable by the second. It had something to do with the fact that Athena couldn't escape him. Apollo shadowed her every breathless step of the way, radiating life and desire. She was Athena, damn it! This couldn't be happening to her.

In the course of her flight, Athena caught glimpses of the Acropolis, the Taj Mahal, Angkor Wat, Tokyo, the Bering Strait, the Grand Canyon, and even more fleetingly, NYC, before she saw that familiar gaping gate and ducked through it. Thanks to a tornado over Kansas, Athena had gained a few seconds on Apollo. She ducked down just inside the fence and held her breath as she heard Apollo's light brisk footfalls swoop into the path.

Out went her arm. Down he crashed. Swiftly she rose. However, as she lifted her foot to spring over him and back out through the gate, Apollo stretched out his strong hand. Upon her slender ankle it fastened.

A decidedly ungraceful 'OOF' escaped from Athena as she belly-flopped on the lawn. Now she was in for it. Only after a great deal of wriggling, kicking, and pinching did Athena break free of the grass—stained wrestling match, but Apollo blocked her escape. She ducked around the picnic table. He countered.

This lunging and darting stalemate lasted several

minutes, encircled the picnic table sometimes at a brisk walk, other moments at a full out dash, and twice detoured beneath the picnic table.

It was the last scramble beneath and scurry around the picnic table that proved fateful. Athena slid just a little as she rose and whipped around to the side. A quarter second at most she lost in speed, but it was enough to enable Apollo to catch her left arm. Immediately, Apollo locked his left hand upon her left forearm and pulled back with all of his might and weight.

Athena tumbled backwards, falling against the far end of the picnic table. As her right arm flailed back, Apollo seized hold of it too, only to be pulled halfway down the length of the picnic table. However, at last, no matter how hard she leaned forward or how mightily she kicked and tried to pull free, Athena was well and firmly anchored, although it took not only all of Apollo's physical mass, but his divine strength to keep her thus ensnared. She pulled. He pulled. Neither budged. In their tug d'amour, a stalemate emerged.

Still, somehow Athena managed to get herself turned about, but still could not break free from Apollo's grip on her wrists.

"This is kismet," said Apollo from between clenched teeth. "We are meant to be."

"The hell we are," Athena growled back as she strained with all of her might.

Freshly washed, Venus sashayed outside. A broad smile brightened her relentlessly lovely face. She stopped beside the picnic table and sized up the situation with her hands propped on her hips. "How's it going?"

Apollo's face reddened as he willed himself to resist Athena's might. "Well, she didn't turn into a tree."

"I told you she wouldn't. Do you need any help?"

Athena snarled at her, but under the circumstances she didn't dare spare so much as a breath to curse out her tormentor, not while Apollo sat braced upon the picnic table pulling on her arms.

"I've got it. Thank you anyway," said Apollo.

"I'll leave you to your wooing." With that she turned away, but stopped and turned back. Veering toward Athena, she said in a tone of mild exasperation, "Oh here. Let me."

Index fingers outstretched, flexed once, twice in preparation, Venus circled behind Athena.

If Athena hadn't had her eyes squeezed shut in the midst of her efforts to out pull Apollo, she might have seen in time. She might have been able to react in time, but she didn't and therefore she couldn't.

Venus poked Athena in her sides.

Athena let out a very female yelp and sprung away from those infernal, ticklish fingers – and into Apollo's embrace.

Venus slapped her hands together and walked away. "There. That did it."

The Goddess of Love returned within without a backwards glance at the astonished and appalled look breathless Athena fixed upon the radiant smile that returned to Apollo's reddened face.

"Together at last," he said.

There was no avoiding bodily contact with him. Not only had Apollo wrapped his arms about her, but his legs too. In order to push away, Athena had to press her forearms against his strong, warm chest and feel the heart pounding within it. Instinct got the better of her. She tried to use her forearms for leverage, but became all to aware of not only the warmth and pounding of his heart, but the sensation that somehow her own heartbeat reverberated through her arms, communicating some message that served only to betray her.

That certainly seemed to be the case, judging by the terrible and beautiful light that filled Apollo's eyes. Apollo pinned her arms behind her back.

Athena writhed, but his grip only tightened. A thorn bush! No. Poison ivy! No. Cactus! No. She was Athena, damn it! There was no way that she was going to turn into a plant. "This can't be happening."

Apollo's breath was on her cheek. "And why shouldn't it?"

With blushing shock, Athena realized that he was nuzzling her. "Because I'm Athena."

"Of that I'm very much aware."

The instant after Athena felt Apollo's right hand tilt her chin, she wondered why she hadn't noticed its absence behind her back. Only his left hand shackled her wrists now. Theoretically, she could yank an arm free and deliver one sound punch, but Apollo's lips were a half a second away from touching hers.

And then, there they were.

And the whole world took a deep breath.

Athena closed her eyes. Apollo closed his. His left hand released her wrists and joined his right hand upon her back. If Apollo's heart possessed wings, they would have burst out of his chest and flown over them with delirious joy when Athena wrapped her arms about his neck.

Hermes stumbled out the back door. He shot a glare back at Medusa as she followed him. "But I went for the gelato already."

"Well, go again."

"Athena dumped the gelato. Make her go." Hermes pointed out the culprit and froze, eyes a-goggle, mouth a-gape. His outrage reduced to an elongated vowel which turned into an 'OW' when Medusa stumbled into him without seeing him.

"Hermes!" snapped Medusa.

Hermes pointed. His mouth opened, but nothing coherent emerged.

"Oh-my-God," said Medusa.

Hermes shook his finger in the couple's direction, desperate to hang onto at least one word in order to spit it out.

Medusa cast wild looks at the sky as she seized hold of Hermes' pointing arm. "I'll go with you."

Although she pulled, Hermes dragged his feet and stared. "But – But – But."

Medusa yanked him out through the gate and pushed him ahead of her down the sidewalk. "Come on. I don't want to be around here when she goes off."

Hermes stumbled back though. "But look at them!"

Medusa grabbed him by the arm and propelled him forward again. "I saw. I saw."

Hermes' voice drifted from down the sidewalk. "But that's impossible, isn't it?"

Medusa's caustic voice replied, "Traffic will be a little more congested en route to Italy, what with all the flying pigs."

One kiss had become two, then three and four, growing longer and longer.

The nightingale was so stunned it fell out of its tree. The neighbor's cat was so distracted too that it failed to notice.

Mars came outside, glanced about for Hermes, saw the impossible, slid down the back steps, and landed hard. He rubbed his eyes and looked again. Nope. He

wasn't imagining it and even as he gawked, Apollo drew
Athena up upon his lap, which she straddled as readily as
Venus did Mars in his own bedroom upstairs. Apollo lay
back and Athena leaned down, drinking each other in
with ravenous kisses.

Wincing, Mars rose and stumbled back inside.
The door closed. It re-opened immediately. "Look for
yourself."

Venus poked her head out. Her face lit up. "This
is wonderful!"

Mars poked his head out. "Gee. I don't know
about that."

Venus trotted out pulling him along behind her.
"Let's go for a walk. I need to find Juliet."

"Why do I have to go?"

"Do you really want to be in the vicinity when
Athena goes off?"

"Excellent point. Let's find Juliet."

Off they set, arm in arm.

Abandoned to their mutual fate, Athena came up
for air and smiling with wonder, slid off the picnic table
to stand again. Apollo's hands rested in her hands as
though they belonged there, and as Athena backed toward the house, she drew him along with her, across the
lawn. Lotuses sprouted beneath their feet and blossomed
in their wake.

The back door made scarcely any sound as Apollo
closed it.

11. Saturday Night in Firenze

Enjoying the sights, sounds, and even the humble jostling mortals, Hermes led the way. Medusa came next excavating with feverish concentration the last of her gelato from its cup with a plastic spoon. Hand in hand, Mars and Venus strolled next, smiling at everything. With her arms folded across her breast and her eyes glancing nervously from side to side, Juliet brought up the rear.

Hermes held his arms up, saluting everything. "And here we are: back in front of the Palazzo Vecchio, right where we started the tour. How do you like Firenze, Juliet?"

"I think I would have like Florence better if we had actually flown here on an actual airplane," she said.

Venus looked back at her. "I thought you were enjoying yourself."

"I was, somewhat, once I got over the shock of it all. One minute I was standing in front of my house asking you what happened to Stewart, and the next we were swooping over the Alps."

"You have to admit that was pretty cool," said Hermes.

"Yes, it was, but a little warning would have been nice."

"I did ask you to go on a little errand with us," said Venus.

"But you didn't give me a chance to say 'yes'."

"I promise next time, Juliet," said Mars, "we'll let you say 'yea' or 'nay' before we carry you off again anyway."

Venus pinched her love's brawny arm. "He's kidding, Juliet."

"What did happen to Stewart?" Juliet looked off to the right at the sculpture of Perseus holding out Medusa's severed head.

Medusa licked off her spoon and tossed it and the cup into the garbage. "Trying to get his brothers out of protective custody, no, actually that would be Udela. Stewart got dragged along. Someone had to drive." She saw the sculpture too and stopped hard.

"Oh, so that's why you came to get me."

"That's right. We weren't taking any chances," said Mars. He grinned at Medusa's seething silence. "Refreshed any memories, Meddles?"

Medusa gave him a scalding look. Her hair wriggled ominously behind her bandanna.

"At least Cellini gave you a pretty face," said Venus. "That Caravaggio made you look so plain that you looked masculine."

"When are we going back?" said Juliet.

"Don't you like it here?" said Venus.

"It's fabulous, but if Stewart were here too..."

Venus reached back and drew Juliet up alongside her, linking arms with her. "I understand."

Amid the steady hum and bustle in the Piazza della Signoria a man bellowed. Mars stopped and frowned into the flowing throngs.

The man hollered again.

Hermes stopped and scanned the crowds too. "That sounded like..."

"My boy!"

Mars looked as though he was about to die.
"Zeus?"

"Oh NO," said Medusa.

"Zeus?" said Juliet, craning for a better look.
"Not the same…?"

"Son!" He emerged fully from the throng with his
arms wide open.

"Dad!" Mars still could not believe his eyes or his
misfortune.

"He looks like Father Christmas," said Juliet.

Hermes grimaced and shook his head. "But only
if Father Christmas had retired to Florida and drank
thirty cans of beer every day."

A tall, full-bellied man strode forth, pinched a
teenage girl in passing, which caused her to squeal, and
took Mars forcefully in his embrace. Leaving one son
winded, Zeus caught his more slippery stripling of a son
in the crook in his arm and roughed up his already
scruffy dark hair.

Hermes winced. As soon as Zeus released him, he
swiped up his cap from where it had fallen on the paving
stones. "Yeah, real nice to see you too," he grumbled.

"What are you doing here?" said Mars.

"My boy, you don't sound happy to see me."

"I wasn't expecting to run into you, that's all."

"Well, here I am." Zeus looked around. "Nice
place. I should get out more often." His glance followed
another gaggle of nubile young maidens in their jeans.

"Where's Mother?" said Mars.

Wild-eyed, Zeus pivoted every which way. "Why?
Where? Did you see her?"

"No. I was just asking."

Zeus sighed and mopped his brow. He looked
frankly relieved, but then he smiled as he saw Venus. He

recoiled a little though when he saw Medusa wrinkling her nose back at him. Then he saw Juliet, a most fetching little morsel of femininity, and his expression brightened. It clouded up again the instant Medusa stepped between them with her arms folded over her breast and her brows lowered over her glowing eyes.

"Where's my darling daughter?" he said.

Mars exchanged silent, strange looks with the rest. "Why do you ask?" he said.

"Everyone else is here," said Zeus. "Where is Athena?"

"Blowing…"

Medusa's palm against the back of Hermes' head shut him up fast.

"Ow." Hermes rubbed the back of his head and gave her a dirty look.

"Uh…" Mars shrugged at Venus. "She's with Apollo."

"I should have figured that," said Zeus. "Thick as thieves those two are."

"Oh you have no idea," said Hermes.

"Where are my two golden ones?" said Zeus.

"Back in Essex," said Mars blandly.

"Oh." Zeus stood looking idle-minded for a moment. Then his glance kindled. "Let's go see them. I haven't seen either of them in centuries. Certainly not since Apollo packed it off to Gandara all those centuries ago."

Venus and Medusa exchanged nervous looks and tried to smile convincingly as they regarded Zeus.

"Actually, they're both a little busy at the moment," said Venus.

"Too busy to see dear old Papa?"

Venus jiggled her head. "Yes. My fault actually. I

got them all tangled up in one of my projects."

Hermes giggled and ignored her warning glance. "Yeah, they're pulling an all-nighter."

"Well. Still. They could use a five or even fifteen minute break, I dare say. Let's go." Zeus caught both of his sons in his oversized arms and beamed at the ladies.

Medusa bit on her nails. Venus swallowed hard, but managed to maintain her pleasant expression. Juliet simply gaped.

"I'll lead the way," Mars said quickly. He managed to pull free, but Hermes remained caught in an iron embrace.

Venus and Medusa seized Juliet's hands.

"Don't worry," said Medusa under her breath. "We won't let him hurt you."

Until that instant, Juliet hadn't really been afraid of that pot-bellied senior citizen. Once forgotten names popped into her head: Europa. Leda. Danae. Ganymede. As the Piazza dissolved into the distance and the stars shone more beautifully than diamonds, she clung tight to her protectresses hands. Below, towns and cities sent their amber glows into the atmosphere, dimly, and then so distinctly that she could pick out streets and buildings, and then again receding in their radiant, polluted fogs back into the night. She didn't remember being able to see the landscape so clearly on the way to Florence. One moment they had been grouped on her front doorstep, hauling her into their midst, and the next they had been standing along the banks of the Arno gazing across toward Santa Croce.

"We're going slower this time," she said aloud.

Venus nodded. "Ares is stalling for time." Then she looked around Juliet to Medusa, exchanging yet another secret look of alarm with the Gorgon.

Not only did Mars make certain that the return flight dragged a little, but he also set them all down several blocks away from Stewart's street directly in front of a pub. Zeus released Hermes from his paternal stranglehold, but scarcely had he a chance to survey his surroundings with a roguish eye when Mars tapped his elbow.

"Care for a pint?" Mars jerked his thumb toward the pub.

Zeus brightened and slapped his belly. Smacking his red, fleshy lips, he said, "Don't mind if I do. A pint or two…"

"…Or four," muttered Medusa.

"…Or more," mumbled Hermes.

"…would just hit the spot. Lead on, Son." Zeus slapped Mars on the shoulder, nearly propelling the formidable War God face first into the pub door.

Recovering his balance and dignity, Mars opened the door for everyone and rolled his eyes for their benefit as soon as Zeus passed him.

Surrounded by so many old faces, Juliet sighed and began to smile. Venus and Medusa released their grip, but they flanked her every step of the way with their stares fixed on Zeus' white head.

"I thought he was moping on Mt. Olympus," Medusa grumbled to Venus.

"I thought he was too," said Venus. "He NEVER leaves Mt. Olympus. What is he doing out here?"

Hermes sidled close to them. "You don't suppose he found his Viagra, do you?"

"Don't be silly," said Venus. "If he had, he'd be humping every woman in sight."

"Where is the 'Big Gun' then?" said Hermes.

"Who knows where Hera is," said Venus.

"I'll guarantee you though that wherever the old boy is the Big Gun won't be far behind. They're both so disfunctionally co-dependant that it isn't funny," said Medusa.

Mars made sure that Zeus had the first pint and dispatched him to find them a booth. The others re-grouped around Mars. He kept an eye on his old man as he handed out the drinks, and Hermes paid for them.

"So what happens now?" said Juliet.

"Hell, if I know," said Hermes.

"One thing's certain," said Mars, "we have to keep him away from Apollo and Athena."

"His precious princess shagging the golden boy would upset him," said Medusa. "Heads would roll. Theirs first most likely."

Venus met Mars' stare. Her eyes widened. "Oh my."

Mars nodded. "Yeah."

"Yeah what?" said Medusa.

Hermes' glance traveled from Mars to Venus. Then he groaned. "This could get very ugly fast."

"What would?" said Juliet.

"Imagine if Athena gets pregnant," said Venus. Her grim expression was sobering to see.

"Knowing what I know about Apollo, she is already," said Hermes.

"He'll eat them both alive!" said Medusa.

"You know it." Mars' eyes followed Zeus across the room.

"He'll be a grandfather. What's the problem with that?" said Juliet.

"You didn't study mythology much, did you?" said Hermes.

"Some. But that was Stewart and Erian's thing

when they were kids."

Mars gave Juliet a genuinely, thoroughly compassionate look. It awed her to see the brash War God show this whole other fraternal side. Suddenly Venus' devotion to him made sense. "A child of their making, Juliet, would be powerful enough to eclipse Zeus utterly. Get it?"

"More than that," said Venus thoughtfully, "a child born of their passion would usher in a whole new age."

"So if he found out?" said Juliet.

"He would destroy them and their child," said Hermes. "He ate Athena's mother because he was told that her unborn child would have the power to overthrow him, but that didn't stop Athena from erupting into being from his forehead."

Mars smiled to himself. "She was always headstrong – no pun intended. You can't stop Athena."

"So what do we do?" said Juliet.

"We make certain that he doesn't find out," said Mars. "I don't work for that old perv anymore and I don't owe him anything either."

"So what's the plan?" said Hermes.

"We keep him distracted until we talk to the two lovebirds," said Mars. "They must be warned."

"But the Delphic Oracle has a big mouth, and when she gets high, she blabs all sorts of nonsense," said Medusa.

"Medusa's right," said Mars. "She won't be able to resist telling Zeus that he's even more obsolete than ever."

Hermes gulped down his pint and wiped off his mouth on his sleeve. "Don't worry. I'll take care of her."

"How?" said Mars.

"I'll tell her that Zeus knows what she did with his Viagra on April Fools' Day."

"But weren't you responsible for that?" said Venus.

"I was, but she doesn't know that. She'll be hiding so deep in the Earth that even Hades won't be able to find her."

"Have fun," said Mars with a wry grin.

"Don't I always?" His cap set at a jaunty angle, Hermes slipped out into the night.

Medusa watched him go. "I still haven't repaid him for the refrigerator incident. Remind me to turn him to stone for an hour when he gets back." Looking idly about, she spied Udela and frowned. "Don't look now, Mars, but there's your old girlfriend."

"Huh? What?" Mars glanced her way. "OH."

"If looks could kill, Mars," said Venus.

"Shit!" Juliet moved beyond Mars. "The last person I ever wanted to see again."

"Patience. Patience," Mars murmured. "Don't panic."

Juliet couldn't be sure whether he spoke to her or to himself.

"Zeus found a booth." Venus sighed and waved back at him. "Come on." She linked her arm through Juliet's and strolled through the crowd. For once, she did not return the bright interested glances that flew her way. Frankly, the Goddess of Love and Beauty looked a little cross, as though braced for a quarrel.

"Watch it." Medusa's eyes flashed flame red at the stranger who nearly knocked her pint out of her hand.

The stranger's eyes went wide. He scrambled out of her range.

As they settled into the booth across from Zeus, he winked at Juliet.

Medusa rattled. Her black mamba locks writhed beneath her blood red bandanna.

Zeus looked away and drank his beer. "Say, Venus darling, who is that voluptuous piece of overripe fruit talking to Ares?"

"THAT is a predatory piece of work named Udela Dunk."

Zeus chortled indulgently at her over his beer. "Was that the tart tone of jealousy I just heard?"

"Not at all."

"You have a rival it seems."

"No more than if he were shagging a blow-up doll," retorted Venus evenly, if a little crisply.

"How is Hera doing?" said Medusa.

" 'Couldn't say. The last I saw her she was off to some sort of empowerment seminar that Artemis arranged."

"So you slipped out of your cage, eh?" said Medusa.

"I went for a little stroll. There's no harm in that."

"Did you ask her for permission first?"

Zeus leveled cold eyes on her. "You look like you could use a haircut, Medusa."

"Watch it, you dirty old man. I don't answer to you. In fact, I never answered to you."

"You answered fast enough when my brother Poseidon called."

"Remind me to introduce you to our new boss real soon."

Zeus took on a look of pure disgust. "It's bad enough that the Delphic Oracle taunts me about it. I don't need some upstart African priestess smarting off…"

"Upstart African priestess? Excuse me, but I'm an incarnation of the primordial creative life force. I'm as old as this beleaguered Earth and that makes me your Elder, so show some respect, or North Pole, Alaska is going to have itself a brand new Santa Claus statue."

"Santa Claus?" Zeus looked down at his gut. "I'm not really that fat, am I?"

"Yeah, you are," said Medusa.

"Well that explains it."

"Explains what?" said Venus.

"All the children in Fort Lauderdale followed me around this morning telling me what they wanted for Christ-Mass."

"Well, that does explain it," said Medusa.

"Explain what?" said Zeus.

"Those clothes. Are you trying to blind people with those colors?"

"Like them?" He beamed down at himself. "I got them in Oahu actually."

Medusa grimaced and shook her head. "Unbeliev-able."

Zeus guzzled down the last of his beer and let go a triumphant belch as he slammed his empty pint on the table. "I could use another pint." Leering, he leaned across the table toward Juliet. "Maybe my son will intro-duce me to his luscious friend. Do you think he will?"

"Miracles do happen," Juliet mumbled.

Venus sat up straight and looked away.

Zeus patted Juliet's hand, oblivious to how swiftly she recoiled from his touch. "That's the spirit." Taking his empty pint with him, Zeus ambled patiently through the clusters of mortals, his white head towering over a dark sea of drab heads.

"I didn't think you were speaking to me, Mrs. Dunk," Mars said, with one eye on the booth where apparently words were being exchanged. So far Zeus seemed to have the upper hand judging by the glowering looks Medusa AND Venus fixed on him, as well as the smirk on Zeus' face.

"I had every right to be furious this morning after what you and your chums did." Udela's gaze wandered the length and breadth of Mars' body.

'Just don't let her touch you. DON'T LET HER TOUCH YOU,' Mars kept thinking.

Her hand brushed over his belt buckle.

He took a step back. " 'Want another pint?" he called over his shoulder.

"Two more please," said Zeus. "I've a raging thirst in me tonight." He appraised Udela as brazenly as she did him. "Raging thirst."

Udela flushed pink from head to toe as Zeus' deep voice rolled over her.

The wave of relief that washed over Mars left him almost weak in the knees. He leaned on the bar and held up three fingers.

Three pints arrived promptly. Zeus handed one to Udela and took the other two. His eyes gleamed.

Udela wriggled on her high heels and simpered. "Thank you, Mister…?"

"Jupiter," said Mars quickly as Zeus opened his mouth. "He's Bill Jupiter."

"Bill?" said Zeus.

"Run with it," Mars hissed over his shoulder.

"Right. Yes. That's me. Bill Jupiter from Jupiter, Florida."

Mars wanted to pound his head on the bar, but

sheer force of will restrained him from doing so. He rolled his eyes toward the ceiling.

"You didn't introduce the lady to me, Son."

"Son? You're his son?" Udela's eyes popped.

"I was adopted," said Mars.

"Ares!"

"I was adopted, right, Bill?" Mars glared back so fiercely that Zeus blinked. There. That settled it.

Zeus shrugged and smiled again at Udela. "I mean, I'm like a father to him. I'm so fond of the boy that I get carried away sometimes. Now, milady, what is your name?"

"Udela Dunk."

"Married?"

"Widowed."

"Join us?"

"I would love to, Bill."

"Follow me then."

Mars ordered a whiskey, downed it on the spot, and then trailed the couple to the booth with his own pint in his hand.

"She's coming to our table?!" Juliet slumped in her seat. "If she says one word to me…"

Venus smiled cunningly at Medusa. "I doubt she'll bother with you now that Zeus is here."

Zeus and Udela slipped in opposite of them.

Mars squeezed in next to Venus and pressed his face against her neck. She stroked his cheek reassuringly.

When Udela finally pried her attention away from Bill Jupiter, she set eyes on Juliet. An expression of cold indifference rose up. "Oh, it's you."

Juliet couldn't touch her pint. "Yes, me. Where's Stewart?"

In a tone of almost blithe indifference, she said, " 'Still sitting at the police station trying to get his brothers released."

"How come you're here then?"

"It didn't make sense having both of us there just sitting on our arses. Besides, I felt the need for some fresh air."

"Fresh air? In a pub? You old slag."

"There, easy now, young Miss. Show some respect for your elders," said Zeus, mimicking Medusa.

"I've had enough," said Juliet. "Let me out."

Venus and Mars got up to let her out.

Medusa scooted out behind her. "Wait for me, Juliet."

Venus exchanged signals with Medusa as she passed. Then she ushered Mars back into the booth and settled nice and cozy next to him. Mars sighed, but Venus showed no trace of boredom or restlessness. Mars didn't feel much like conversing, and Venus wasn't inclined to talk, being too interested in watching destiny unfold as Udela's hand worked its sinuous progress up Zeus' thigh.

12. Sunday Morning and Other Complications

Morning found Mars, Venus, Medusa, and Hermes ranged about their sturdy old picnic table keeping double vigil on their freshly renovated abode and the trembling hull that was the Dunk residence. Juliet slept on the picnic bench beneath her jacket. Mars and Venus listened to the laborious grunts and groans and excruciating moans reverberating through Udela's windowpanes. Mars looked as though he'd rather have his teeth knocked out with a hammer, but Venus sat smiling and kicking her feet. Hermes and Medusa found the strange light radiating from Athena's bedroom window absolutely mesmerizing.

From that upstairs window a peculiar amber glow emanated, fading in and out and shifting to and fro, as rhythmic as pacing. Then, slowly, it filled the window and blazed out steady and strong, and alarmingly red.

"Oooooh," went Hermes and Medusa.

Venus looked over her shoulder. "Hello, Nirvana."

Mars glanced once. "We may not see either of them for a year."

"Oh dear. That would be my fault again," said Venus. "I did loan Apollo that book on Tantra a month ago, so there is no telling. Ah well. What happens happens."

Both regarded the Dunk household again.

At last silence came from the Dunk household,

just as the sun's first light broke across the horizon and the glow faded from Athena's bedroom window. Off to the side the work shed door opened. Apollo emerged with Athena warm in his embrace.

Hermes and Medusa gawked.

The strange reddish glow flared up again and the curtains moved as though someone had brushed past them.

"Wait a minute!" Hermes pointed from the window to the divine couple, both of whom jumped at the sound of his voice. "If you're down here, who's in that bedroom?"

"Who's where?" Athena said once she'd got over the surprise of seeing everyone looking at them.

"Up there." Hermes pointed.

"You were both down there all night?" said Medusa.

Venus and Mars shifted so that they could watch both the Dunk house and the divine couple.

"Yes, for the most part," said Apollo.

"Where's the bull?" said Mars.

"Sent it back across the Irish Sea to Tara, where it belonged, before another feud got started," said Apollo.

Athena turned and gawked at the window.

Apollo followed her glance. "What the hell...?"

Athena turned. "I knew it! I told you my room was haunted. Didn't I say I felt someone watching us last night?"

"So it wasn't the electrical wiring after all," he said. "What do you know about that? Well, I suppose next time we could repair to my chamber."

"No way," said Athena.

"What do you mean: no way?"

"Because there's a ghost of an ax murderer in

there," she said.

They all looked aghast.

"Where do you think that weird smell comes from?" Athena added.

"How come you never saw it?" Hermes demanded.

Apollo glanced at the house and paled a little. "Because I was only in there long enough to change clothes. I haven't even taken a nap in my room, thanks to that mushroom stew Friday night."

"That explains why no one ever lived there for long all these years," said Mars.

"It's hiding under his bed actually. You have to look for it. When I dropped a pencil, I spied the wretched ghoul and his bloody ax and wished I hadn't," said Athena.

Apollo whipped out a cell phone from his back pocket.

"Who are you calling?" said Mars.

"Hades." Apollo headed into the house, still talking, "Hades! You old son… "

Mars got down off of the picnic table. "Come on, Love. Let's go see how Stewart is doing."

"Very well," Venus sighed. She shuffled alongside him.

Medusa climbed off the picnic table next, groaned and stretched. "Come on, Hermes."

"Come on where?" he said.

"To get the Sunday papers. Oh! And milk and some more eggs too. You want breakfast, don't you?"

"Oh, all right. Coming." Hermes bounced off the picnic table and sauntered after her.

"Watch over Juliet, will you, Athena?" Venus called.

Athena glanced over at Juliet's sleeping form. "Certainly."

Venus and Mars strolled off in one direction.

Medusa and Hermes slouched off in the other.

Athena shuffled toward the picnic table and frowned a little as she rubbed her belly. When she had climbed up and settled herself comfortably on the table's end, she discovered that she was a little bloated. She patted her tummy, made a face, and then shrugged. "'Must have been something I ate," she murmured.

Apollo came back out. Athena could just make out Hades' voice venting on the cell phone. Judging by the manner in which Apollo rolled his eyes, the Lord of the Underworld was on a tangent. She could just guess.

"Look. I've got some more renovations to do as soon as Mars and Hermes turn up so I've got to go. Just send the Ferryman around with his cattle prod and get these nuisances out of here. Right. Yes. We'll talk later." A huge exasperated sigh escaped Apollo as he hung up and closed the phone.

Another, softer sigh escaped him as he sat between Athena's knees, rested his arms on her thighs and laid his head back against her stomach. The moment he felt her fingers stroking his hair, he closed his eyes. "Persephone's gone off to visit her mother and he's in a sulk."

"You'd think he'd be used to it by now."

Apollo nodded. "However, I'm beginning to understand. He's also still sore that Hera took his dog."

Juliet stirred and sat up.

Apollo beamed at her. "Morning. 'Sleep tolerably well?"

Juliet rubbed her eyes and shivered. "Tolerably. Did Stewart come back?"

"You would've known first if he had, Dear," said Athena.

"He's bound to show up soon, right?" said Juliet.

Athena nodded.

"I'm famished," said Juliet. "Do you have any toast?"

Apollo stood up and began to head inside. "We have toast, jam, oatmeal, sausage, bacon, a couple of eggs left, waffle mix... Have a preference?"

"Toast and eggs perhaps, if it isn't too inconvenient?"

"Scrambled, sunny side up…?"

"Scrambled and well-browned if you please."

"And what would you like?" Apollo smiled sweetly at Athena.

Athena sat with her hand pressed to her stomach. She looked perplexed and even a little confounded that she was perplexed in the first place.

"Surely you have an appetite, especially after last night," he added.

"I do, but I am so absolutely starved that I can't decide what I do want."

"You'll have to make up your mind, Athena. Unlike Shiva, I don't have the advantage of sprouting extra arms when I need them." He winked at Juliet. "Can you just see that?"

"Actually, I can," she said.

"Narrowed it down yet, dearest?" said Apollo.

Athena slapped her hands upon her knees. "Yes! I want my eggs scrambled with cheese and chives on top. I want two waffles, well-browned, with maple syrup and jalapenos."

"Jalapenos?" he said.

"And plenty of pepper on my eggs. And cactus

jelly."

"Cactus Jelly?"

"I want oatmeal with brown sugar and cinnamon. Oh! And sausage – with hash browns, plenty of pepper there too."

Apollo tore his frowning glance away from Athena to regard Juliet. "Anything to drink?"

"Tea will be fine," said Juliet.

"Tea for me too," said Athena, "and some chocolate milk, and can you mix up some of that pomegranate, citrus punch, and ruby red grapefruit punch like we had yesterday?"

"Yes. Give me a few minutes." He turned to go inside, an odd expression upon his face.

"Oh!" Athena waved her hand in the air. "One last thing! Pickles – a big jar of kosher pickles. I'm just so hungry today."

Apollo froze in mid-step. He glanced back, more than a little wide-eyed. "No kidding." He had one foot inside the back door when Medusa came traipsing back, swinging a grocery bag. Hermes sauntered along behind her with all of the morning papers under his arm. "Hermes!"

Hermes ducked behind the fence.

"I saw you," said Apollo.

Hermes glanced over the top of the fence.

Apollo wriggled his finger at him. "I got a shopping list."

"Man, do I look like an errand boy to you?"

To which Medusa and Apollo AND Athena replied – in unison – "YES."

The fists Hermes clenched at his sides, the thunderclouds darkening upon his brows, all betrayed the tantrum seething beneath the surface. Of course the stomping was to be expected, as was the energy with which Hermes folded his arms over his puffed out chest, and the brisk tapping coming from his right foot.

"I need these things, so you have to beat it out to New Mexico – "

"New Mexico?!"

"Look in Texas, wherever, but I need jalapenos and cactus jelly, and I also need maple syrup, kosher pickles, chives, potatoes, and cinnamon."

"What are you working on? A case of indigestion?"

"Just get those things, you cattle rustler, and be back as soon as you can."

"You just won't let it go, will you? I was young then, and you got your cows back."

"Once a juvenile delinquent, always a juvenile delinquent. Now go!" Apollo pointed.

Hermes did not notice the odd look Apollo cast toward Athena. He slapped the newspapers atop his favorite barrel seat. Mumbling rudely as he stomped off preoccupied him too much.

Apollo called out the back door. "Hey, Medusa!"

"What, Sunshine?" she said.

Apollo poked his head out. "Give me a hand in the kitchen?"

"Me? What about…?" Medusa pointed in Athena's direction.

Apollo shook his head with such sudden vehemence that Medusa choked off the last word upon her tongue.

"All right." She followed him inside with her groceries. Although Athena's stare reeked of indifference, Medusa gave her the most innocuous, if tight, little smile possible, but then her glance landed on Udela's bedroom window. "Oh! There's something I need to tell you."

The door shut behind them.

"You aren't really going to eat all that?" said Juliet.

Athena went wide-eyed with astonishment that Juliet even asked such a question. "Of course I am. I'm famished, which is rather surprising, as my tummy feels rather odd today."

Distracted again by her worsening hunger, Athena rubbed her hand against her belly, its softly rounded mound protruding ever more gradually.

Juliet stared though and really began to be concerned. Somehow she didn't think it right to mention it, so she changed the subject. "Do you mind if I ask you a personal question?"

Athena looked at her. Her gaze turned piercing. She waited.

"You both said a lot of things to me, and I'm still trying to wrap my mind around it. Was it true? All of it? I mean, I didn't hallucinate any of this, did I?"

Athena frowned a little, but still looked pleasantly upon her. "What did you think you hallucinated?"

"You are the real Athena?" said Juliet.

"Umhmmm." Athena smiled as she nodded once.

"And Phoebus is Phoebus Apollo."

Athena's smile traveled from Juliet toward the windows. She could just make Apollo out past the curtains. She sighed. "None other."

Juliet glanced toward Udela's darkened window. "Isn't Zeus your father? I mean both of you?"

Athena looked down at her and still smiled. "So they say."

"But – I know you're gods and all – but isn't that still incest?"

Athena looked about them. Her gaze lingered

upon a cloud idling in the sky. Then she shifted down to sit beside Juliet. "What I am about to tell you isn't commonly known."

"It's a secret then."

"No. Just extremely obscure." Athena took a firm breath. "Zeus is not my father. Did you tell Stewart what we told you yesterday?"

Juliet hesitated, but finally nodded.

"Did he believe you?"

"Let's say that he didn't look all that surprised."

"Clever lad that Stewart is."

"Didn't you spring from Zeus' head?"

"Like a bad idea. It was all sleight of hand really. Honestly, since when is anyone born from someone's head, and a man's head too? Think about it."

"I see what you mean," said Juliet. "So Metis isn't your mother either."

"Impossible. Zeus had digested her."

"Ugh. That's disgusting."

"Tell me about it. I had to pretend that monster was my Daddy. He still thinks he's my Pa. Ignorance is bliss."

Juliet cast another worried glance at that bedroom window. She kept her voice low. "Who are you then?"

"Athena is but one of my names."

"What are they?"

Athena smiled.

"You won't tell me," said Juliet. "All right. Where are you really from?"

"Long before I was patroness of Athens, Crete was my domain. I am Minoan and was so long before that ogre Kronos fathered Zeus on Rhea."

"Why pretend?"

"I had, and still have, a mission: to help humanity.

However, if I came into the Pantheon as an utter out-
sider, I wouldn't have enjoyed as much influence as I
have. Certainly Zeus would've curtailed my power and
raped me into the bargain, but as 'Daddy's Girl'…"

Juliet smiled and nodded. "You were untouch-
able."

"I am still protected as long as Zeus never finds
out that I'm an interloper from Crete."

"Does anyone else know?"

Athena frowned at the horizon. "I think Venus
does."

"And you aren't worried that she'll tell?"

"She's sitting on it until she wants something from
me. Apollo knows too, but for all intents and purposes
he's a changeling too."

"A changeling?"

"He isn't from the Mediterranean at all, but then
you can tell that just by looking at him." Athena tugged
at a lock of her own lustrous hair.

"Where did he come from then?"

"Golden boy is Nordic. Still, he and Venus have
always had this odd, reluctant bond between them, so I
think he's spent some time east of wherever Venus sailed
from. She claims to be from Cyprus, but I have my suspicions that she came from someplace in Asia."

"How come this isn't common knowledge?"

"Because the Greeks and then the Romans so
thoroughly co-opted us that most traces of our original
incarnations were bleached away, if not buried entirely."

"You came here for Stewart." Juliet mused over it
all for a moment.

"And for you. Reassuring, isn't it? Sometimes the
cries of despair that one's soul makes are not just heard,
but heeded, and thus our motley crew was dispatched to

this pastoral site."

Juliet snorted. "I've heard many things said about this neighborhood, but never 'pastoral'."

"Compared to some places it would be. Damn!" She rubbed her tummy. "Where's breakfast?"

At that moment Apollo came outside and, tearing his serious and wary glance from the Dunk residence, scanned all four horizons.

Hermes' voice came from the immediate vicinity. "Incoming!"

Apollo ducked as a canvas shopping bag flew over the fence – and landed on Medusa, just as she ventured outside. She fell backwards with the bag clutched to her belly.

Both caught the merest glimpse of Hermes sailing past on the sidewalk.

Medusa pushed the bag aside and leapt to her feet. "That does it! I'm making a fountain ornament out of that whelp."

The next instant they saw Hermes blurring past. Medusa charged mere inches after him. Her taloned fingers stretched out to catch his shirt collar. They heard a raucous crash and heard Hermes yelp, which was followed by the sounds of her kicking what turned out to be the neighbor's shed. "Come out from under there!"

Apollo shrugged, picked up the canvas bag, and after giving his sweetheart a fresh smile and Udela's window a dark look, returned inside to finish making breakfast.

After two more clamorous kicks that caused the neighborhood dogs to bark, Medusa came stomping back, hissing out vague threats under her breath. She slammed the back door behind her.

Even Athena flinched. "Mental note: 'Steer clear

of Medusa today'."

Hermes' head popped up over the fence. His eyes were wide and wild, but his brows had an insolent arch to them. "Where's Medusa?"

"Inside helping Apollo," said Athena.

Hermes plopped down beside Juliet.

"Aren't you afraid of Medusa?" said Juliet.

"Only if she catches me, and she can't."

"She could sneak up on you though," said Athena.

Hermes whipped about. "Ha. Ha. Funny, Athena." He plopped down again, leaned back and stretched his legs out.

The back door opened. Out emerged Apollo and Medusa with two large, rather Arthurian-round, table-sized trays, dangerously laden.

"Already?" Juliet blinked at the feast.

"The advantage of being a deity," said Athena.

"Toast and eggs for you, Miss Paulet," said Apollo.

"Thank you."

"And the rest is yours, Miss Piggy," said Medusa.

Apollo and Medusa laid plate after plate before Athena, piled prettily with everything she requested.

"Watch your hands, Apollo," said Medusa. "She might mistake your fingers for sausages and eat them."

Indeed, Athena had already chomped down half a sausage. "Where's the tea?"

"In a minute, your Majesty." Medusa backed away with a bow, but as she turned to go inside, Athena called after her.

"Can I have mine in a tall glass with sugar, lemon, and lots of ice – please?"

Medusa's step faltered, but she resumed walking with her head bent forward, resembling a bull charging a toreador.

When she returned, Medusa bore a third tray laden
with the required Brown Betty teapot, several cups, no
saucers – thanks to Mars again – and one tall and very
stout Mason jar that jingled softly with ice cubes in am-
ber-colored tea. She set the tray down and set the
remaining Mason jar quite firmly before Athena, and
promptly found herself rooted to the spot beside Apollo,
watching in amazement as Athena cleaned off the first
plate and set her knife and fork to work on the next
plate.

"What's gotten into her?" said Medusa.

"Well…" said Apollo.

"Besides you."

"I'm afraid that may be the point," Apollo muttered.

"Oh. OH!" Medusa's eyes popped. "Already?"
She and Hermes shot wary looks at the Dunk house.

"Uh oh," mumbled Hermes. "What do we do?"

"We don't panic," said Medusa. "Right, Apollo?"

"Indeed," said Apollo. His glance traveled from
his divine consort to Udela's window and back again.

Ponderous snoring began to rattle Udela's windowpanes.

All three deities sighed with relief. Hermes retreated inside.

Venus and Mars came back.

Mars' pace quickened. He let go of Venus' hand.
"Breakfast! Good. I'm starving."

Venus veered off to the side of the picnic table
and motioning behind her, gave Juliet a bright, affirming
smile. 'He's coming', she mouthed.

Mars headed straight for one of the overloaded
plates, his hand outstretched to grab a nibble. Athena
snarled at him, literally. He whipped his hand out of

range at once and crossed around to stand behind
Apollo.

"There's more on the stove," said Apollo.

"Right." Mars rushed inside.

Medusa frowned. "Hey, slow down before you
choke, Athena."

Athena took time enough to give her one malin-
gering look as she set aside another emptied plate and
drew the next into place. "I'm hungry."

"You've completely lost it, girl."

"Oh, lay off and hand me the pepper mill."

Medusa edged it closer. Athena snatched it up at
once and liberally ground up fresh pepper all over her
scrambled eggs.

Venus tapped Juliet lightly on the shoulder and
gestured toward the fence just as Stewart strolled into
view. His head was bent forward. His hands were
shoved into his pockets, but he didn't look glum at all. If
anything, Stewart wore a bemused grin.

"Stewart!" cried Juliet.

His pace quickened, as did his grin, turning into a
bright smile. The minute he reached Juliet he bent down
and kissed her cheek and rested his hands on her slender
shoulders. "Breakfast!"

Apollo motioned toward the back door. "There's
plenty on the stove. Help yourself."

Stewart, though, was watching Athena's ravenous
progress. "Are you all right?"

"Ignore her," said Medusa.

"What happened last night?" said Juliet.

"Well…" Stewart began.

Aiken and Erian came into view. Both looked a
little ragged. Aiken wore clothes borrowed from a jani-
tor. Fury boiled beneath the surface, both darkening and

reddening Aiken's face. He stole a glance in their direction, saw the innocent look Venus feigned, and remembered. There she was, the person who had ruined his life.

Erian stared directly ahead. His expression was like one shell-shocked to the point that he fully expected the world about him to degenerate into a Salvador Dali landscape with himself stuck somehow in mid-air above it, trapped forever there doubting everything he saw or felt. He dared not look in his neighbors' direction for fear that they would turn into El Greco-esque aliens or that his house would vanish. Aiken stopped in the gaping gate, but Erian ducked inside their home.

Mars returned with two plates, brimming with breakfast, and sat at the end of the picnic table furthest away from Athena.

Athena cleaned off her last dish, looked longingly at Mars' plates and belched. "I'm still hungry."

Mars edged his plates closer and leaned over them. "Mine."

"But I want seconds."

"Seconds?!?" said Medusa.

Apollo sighed. "Come inside, and if there isn't enough, I'll make more."

With a haste that dazzled, Athena stacked all of her plates and hurried inside just behind Apollo. Her place at the table was immaculate.

Although the insanity had ended with the sunrise, Aiken recognized that he had become a pariah. Every look he had received on the long march home was an unfriendly one. The women who had pursued him mere hours before with feverish eyes hated him now a hundred times more than they had ever desired him. Every man who used to be his mate down at the pub only wanted to catch him alone in an alley as soon as possible. "I'll bet you're pleased with yourself," he said.

Venus made no pretence of her disdain. Her gaze had about as much warmth as a block of Antarctic ice. A more sensible mortal would have backed off immediately.

"Did you tell him?" said Aiken.

"No," she said coolly.

"Was there something I needed to know?" said Mars between bites.

"I would say so," said Aiken.

"Like what?" Mars' fork stood suspended over his plate as his gaze passed from Aiken to Venus.

"Something of a personal nature." Aiken stood with his gaze locked with Venus' stare. He smiled tightly. "Guess who your lady spent the Friday night with?"

"You?" said Mars. He shoveled another bite into his mouth. "Am I right?"

"Well...yes. You don't seem surprised."

Mars shrugged. "Not really. Look, I'm passionate about her, but everyone knows what a serene-faced hussy she is. Well, you are."

Venus sputtered for a response, but words failed her. She settled on folding her arms over her chest and pacing. All the while she cast baleful looks at both Mars and Aiken.

The matter might have dried up and blown away, but Aiken saw Stewart standing still behind Juliet and she nestling in his embrace. "You!"

Juliet bristled. "What?"

"This is all because of you, isn't it?" said Aiken.

"You'd be half right, son," said Mars.

"We came for Stewart," said Venus. "You were just in the way."

"As usual," commented Medusa.

Venus smiled at Medusa and took on a meaningful look. "Oh, you have no idea, Medusa."

"Then enlighten me," said Medusa.

She draped her arm about Medusa's shoulders. "That's right. You haven't heard what he did yet."

"Athena hinted at something reprehensible." Medusa narrowed her eyes at Aiken.

Venus met Juliet's glance.

Juliet squeezed Stewart's hands and rested her face against his right arm. Around it she peered at the cunning smile Venus wore.

"Aiken and Udela drove Juliet away," Venus was saying.

Stewart half-lunged toward Aiken, but Venus stretched out her hand and stayed him with a cunning smile.

"In particular what you did to Juliet was utterly vile." The fierce glance she turned to Medusa said it all.

Medusa's eyes flamed. She advanced toward him. "Aiken, it's time we had a little chat."

Aiken backed toward the gaping gate. Home was so near and still so far away.

Medusa came forward, her shoulders and head bent forward, looking frighteningly like the lionesses on those nature documentaries that Erian was addicted to. As soon as he had both feet beyond the gate, he dashed toward home, but Medusa leapt over his fence and blocked off his own gateway. Her eyes glowed orange. He tried to slip around her for the front door, but she blocked his path again and smiled.

"Aiken Dunk, you are a foul specimen of manhood, and it is time you made amends," said Medusa.

Aiken turned to run.

Medusa was on him in an instant. Just around the

side of their abode the deities heard Aiken's yell of surprise. Then there followed a very solid silence broken abruptly by some rather merry whistling, a rather cavalier melody full of sangfroid. Thus serenading herself, Medusa returned, skipping lightly, back to the picnic table. There she sat at the opposite end from Mars and beamed upon the assembly. "I enjoyed that," she declared.

Carrying a plate, Hermes ventured over to the fence for a peek. "Medusa?"

"Yes?"

Hermes gave her the thumbs up. "Excellent work."

Medusa bowed. "Thank you. Thank you."

Hermes returned to the table. "Time for breakfast."

Athena came outside stretching her back.

Stewart crossed her path. He peered over the fence. "What the Hell!"

"What?" said Juliet.

"She turned Aiken into a statue."

Juliet darted over to look. "Oh my God! She did!"

Both cast fearful looks toward Medusa and her satisfied smile.

"What's with the funny face, Athena?" said Mars.

"I feel odd."

"You are odd," said Medusa.

"Seriously. I feel strangely bloated."

Venus stared. "That's because you are bloated, Athena."

"What?"

Venus stepped up and, pulling Athena's overlong work shirt tight, laid her right hand upon a shockingly well-rounded belly.

Athena let out a cry of disbelief, "No – No." She laid her hands over her belly and pressed in. The mound felt quite firm and, worse, alive under her hands. "This can't be."

Venus took her arm and steered her toward the house. "I think you could use a lie down."

Apollo ventured outside again.

Athena lunged at him. "You!"

Apollo jumped.

"This is your doing!" If it hadn't been for Venus' firm grip on her arm, Athena would have been all over him.

Apollo darted around behind Mars and waited.

"Now. Now," said Venus in a calming tone. "You mustn't excite yourself. Come inside."

Halfway in tears, Athena shook her fist at him. "I'll get you for this. Look at me. I'm emotional."

"That's just your hormones, dear. It's perfectly natural," said Venus.

"I'll get you for this, Apollo." Athena went inside, sniffling.

Apollo breathed a sigh of relief.

Venus came back out.

"How is she?" said Apollo.

"Lying d – " she began.

Athena marched back outside with a box of crackers in her clutches. She was her old calm self again.

"Are you all right?" said Apollo.

Athena gave him a wide-eyed look. "Oh! That! I'm fine now." She shoved another round cracker in her mouth and crunched on it.

Venus shook her head. "I'm keeping an eye on you, Athena."

"What for? I'm fine."

Stewart edged nearer to them. "Is he going to stay like that?"

"Who?" said Athena.

"Aiken."

Athena walked over for a look and gave off a snort of amusement. "The Date Rape Avenger strikes again." She gave Medusa the thumbs up before she shoved another cracker into her mouth.

"Is he stuck like that?" said Stewart.

"Um hmm," went Medusa.

"Serves him right." Juliet returned to her breakfast.

"Whatever shall I tell Mum?" Stewart scratched his head. "No, I can't tell her. Maybe I should tell Erian and let him tell her? You think so?"

Athena nearly choked on her cracker, but recovered. Grinning, she motioned to Apollo and Venus. "I have an idea."

Apollo and Venus approached.

"Venus, go tell Erian that Aiken wants to see him."

"Go quietly," said Medusa under her breath.

"Right." Venus marched across the way.

"Apollo, stand by," said Athena.

Apollo leaned on the fence and feigned utter boredom.

"Watch this." Athena winked at Stewart and crunched on another cracker.

Venus peeked through the kitchen window and knocked gently on the back door.

Erian peeked out past a curtain and hid again.

"I saw you, Erian. Come out. Aiken wants you."

Erian opened the back door just wide enough for his face. "Tell him to come here."

"He can't. He's in a fix and he needs you."

"Where is he?" Erian edged outside.

Venus nodded in the direction of the sidewalk. "On the corner the last I saw him. You'd better hurry. He's in a foul mood after last night."

"And who's to blame for that?"

Venus smiled. "Yeah, but I'm not the one he's going to clobber this time." She turned and casually returned to her own yard, where she too leaned ever so indolently against the fence.

Not daring to remove his gaze from tormentors, Erian crept out onto the sidewalk and grumbling more incoherently than before, headed for the corner. He hesitated though when his gaze met Athena's.

For her part, Athena smiled and nodded once. "Mornin' ", she said, and popped another cracker in her mouth.

Stricken silent, Erian quickened his pace past the gaping gate where Athena and Apollo loitered.

They waited – one second, two, three... Blam! Erian had hurtled through the gate before they quite realized he'd returned.

"Mum!!!" Bang! The back door slammed behind him. "Mum!!!" He bounded upstairs.

"Quick!" Athena nudged Apollo with her foot. "Change him back."

Apollo darted down the sidewalk, a wild grin illuminating his face. He returned almost immediately and resumed his previous stance, as blasé as ever.

Medusa and Hermes exchanged worried looks with Mars.

"He's going to wake Zeus up," said Medusa.

"Oh shit," grumbled Mars. "We'll be fine. We'll be fine. Everyone, stay cool."

They heard Udela complaining all the way down the stairs, and then she emerged, still fastening up her scarlet robe. "You had better have a good reason for waking us up."

Aiken stumbled back up the sidewalk. He had to lean against the fence a moment.

"See what they did to Aiken." Erian hustled Udela as far as the gate. "Now, you have to believe me."

"Believe you about what?" Where is Aiken?"

"He's on the corner. He's been turned to stone, Mum!"

Aiken held his head in his hands and shook it as though trying to shake off a fog in his mind.

"What rubbish. There is your brother," said Udela.

"What?" said Erian.

"He looks fine to me," his mother added.

"But…"

"It's enough, Erian. No more of this foolishness." Udela turned to go back in, but stopped, her glance snagged upon Mars' lazy grin. "I believe you were going to repair the damage you did yesterday."

"Yes, ma'am. As soon as we've finished break-fast." Mars smiled with bright, masculine charm.

Udela frowned from him to Apollo and Hermes, both of whom took on ridiculously innocent smiles. One harrumph and she had shut her back door behind her. They heard her heavy steps climbing the stairs.

Mars sighed. Zeus hadn't come outside. Perhaps he was still sound asleep. Sure enough, the snoring resumed as before.

Aiken stopped at the gate beside Erian. "What are you gawking at?"

"You were solid stone not two minutes ago."

Aiken flinched. The fog was gone. His glance snapped in Medusa's direction. "I was?"

Erian jiggled his head up and down. "You were, I swear."

Medusa smiled prettily and waved her elegant, long fingers at Aiken. Then her eyes narrowed and began to glow orange again.

"I believe you." Aiken started to veer toward the sanctuary of his home, but a flash from Medusa's eyes caused him to change both his mind and his direction. Perhaps he could duck in through the front door.

Medusa arched her brow at Athena.

Athena exchanged salutes with her and exchanged grins with Apollo.

Medusa sped out after him.

There was another horrified yell before Medusa returned, securing her bandanna. She paused to smile and wink at Erian and went back into their own abode, whistling again.

Erian peered around the house. He tensed, but then he slumped and feigned resignation until he had his hand on his own back door. In an instant, he rushed inside and locked the door behind him.

Apollo ducked out through the gaping gate.

Again, they heard a great commotion as Erian went tearing up after his mother and then herding her downstairs. This time they heard Erian prodding Udela out through the front door.

Apollo sauntered back, planted a kiss on Athena's cheek, and leaned upon the fence once more.

Udela's angry voice cracked like a whip. "That's it! I've had enough of this." She marched back in, dragging Erian by his ear. It was hard to say which emotion weighed heaviest on her face, exasperation or disappointment.

Erian struggled. "Ow! Let go. I swear, he WAS a statue a minute ago!"

She paused long enough to shake a finger at Apollo and Mars. "I want my house set to rights by the time I return."

"Yes, ma'am," said Mars as he wiped his mouth on his napkin. Then he exchanged grins with Hermes.

"Where are you going?" said Apollo.

"To get my son admitted," she spat. The door slammed behind Udela and the flailing Erian.

"Poor Erian," said Athena without the slightest trace of sympathy. She polished her nails on her shirt and strutted inside.

Aiken staggered toward his back door, but stopped to look around. " I thought I heard Mum. Where is she?"

Apollo took on a brogue and circled his finger next to his temple. "Inside, but your brother Erian's a wee bit distracted, laddie, so I think she's going to go off to get him admitted."

Medusa came outside with her own plate of breakfast. "I guess that leaves you alone with me, lover boy." She batted her eyelashes at Aiken.

Quick as a flash, Aiken barricaded himself inside his house. They knew he was building a barricade by the great noise he was making just inside the house.

"Hermes, as soon as you've finished, I need you to go get a garage door opening kit," said Mars.

Hermes arched his brows. "A garage door opening kit?"

"An industrial sized one." Mars smiled.

Hermes chortled and attacked his breakfast with greater haste.

Genuinely concerned this time, Juliet and Stewart exchanged looks.

Nothing but noise came from inside the Dunk household.

The snoring stopped. Substantial footsteps descended the stairs and the back door opened. Zeus blinked at the morning light and, closing the door behind himself, said, "Don't mind me, son. I smell sausage and coffee."

They could hear Aiken dashing upstairs and slamming his own bedroom door shut.

Zeus saw the other five deities gawking at him. "Morning, all. Apollo, my boy, come and greet your dear old Dad."

Apollo stood frozen to the spot. Inwardly, he willed Athena to stay out of sight. Under his breath, he muttered, "God, help us."

13. Hera: The Big Gun Is Reloaded

In Udela's absence, it pleased Zeus to idle away the morning at the picnic table cleaning off plate after plate of food that Venus served him. Although he kept bidding Athena to come out and greet him properly, she stayed within, preferring to wave innocently through the kitchen window while she kept the food coming. Whenever Zeus had tried to go inside, either Medusa or Venus blocked his entrance, the former with glowing orange eyes, a forbidding expression, and ominous words about 'wet paint', and the latter with either a fresh cup of coffee or a plate of steaming hot food, and a firm hand on his elbow with which she steered him back to the picnic table.

As soon as Udela had left, dragging her wretched middle son behind her, Mars, Hermes, and Apollo had ducked into Udela's house. None of his boys had poked so much as a nose out since, but a steady racket issued from next door. Finally, Zeus couldn't help being bored.

From their open back door, Medusa and Venus eyed Zeus.

"We're never going to get rid of him," grumbled Medusa. "You realize that, don't you?"

"We have to do something," Athena hissed urgently from deep inside the kitchen. "I'd swear I'm getting bigger by the minute. If he sees me…"

"We won't let him see you," said Medusa, glancing over her shoulder, but she paused to stare. "Good Lord, you ARE getting bigger." She ducked inside.

"What?" said Athena. "But I thought I was just imagining it."

Still standing guard in the doorway, Venus watched Medusa place her hands on Athena's belly, measuring its girth with widening eyes. "Is she larger?" she whispered.

Looking a little alarmed, Medusa nodded.

"What am I going to do?"

Seeing the Goddess of Wisdom nearly fly into a hand flapping panic terrified Venus and Medusa.

"We stay calm," said Venus. "I'll figure out a way to get rid of him, or at least see to it that he's preoccupied."

"What's he doing now?" said Athena.

"He's decided to read the papers," said Venus. "He just picked up the Times."

"What's keeping Udela anyhow?" said Athena. "If she'd just come back, that randy old sod would be out of our hair."

"She's having Erian put away, remember?" said Medusa.

"How long does it take to throw someone in the loony bin anyway?" cried Athena.

"It takes time to fill out the paperwork," said Medusa.

"Calm down, Athena," whispered Venus. "If Zeus hears your voice, he might get curious enough to push his way in, and none of us want that, not while you're in such a vulnerable state."

Athena grabbed a carrot off of the chopping board and chomped on it, while with her free hand, she distractedly rubbed her belly. Between bites, she uttered, "We need to come up with a plan that'll get Zeus off our backs for ages to come."

"Agreed," said both Medusa and Venus.

"We could send him on an errand for the time being." Athena resumed chopping carrots for their lunch.

The other two looked at her.

"So far, all we have for lunch is chopped carrots," said Athena. "We'll give him a honking big list of groceries, and that'll get him out of our hair for at least an half hour."

"Good thinking." Venus ducked inside. "Man the door, Medusa."

"Right." Medusa returned to the doorway, where she leaned with her arms folded across her chest and her seemingly idle gaze focused on Zeus.

Five minutes later, Medusa withdrew inside, and Venus bounced brightly into the doorway, wafting a sheet of paper. "Zeus? Could you do me a little favor?"

It worked. Eager for lunch, Zeus took the prodigious list and ambled off, whistling.

Even the birds breathed a sigh of relief, until…

Out of the stillness, Mars' voice rang out, "Okay! Now try it."

First came the grind of a strangulated doorbell. From the front of the Dunk house issued a terrific rumble and clatter. The whole house vibrated and shivered dust. Aiken dashed outside through the back door with his arms over his head. Venus shook her head and went back inside.

Mars shouted again. "Hold it. Hermes, a little more oil please."

"Bloody Hell." Aiken checked to make certain that the infernal bitch with the serpentine locks wasn't outside also. Then he veered to the gate and peered 'round the side. "What the hell are you doing?"

Mars came around to his side of the house and leaned upon the gatepost. "Just finishing the last bit of renovation."

Medusa came outside, but she was too busy looking behind her to bother with Aiken.

Aiken ducked low and, despite the imminent peril, retreated back inside his groaning house.

Mars grinned at Aiken's panic. He raised his voice again, "All right. Try it again. I think we have it this time."

The doorbell resounded bright and clear and then a more orderly churning and whirring sound disturbed the morning quiet. The Dunk house vibrated only moderately. There was a brief pause.

"One, two, three, four, five," said Mars, "and 'close Sesame'."

The whirring metallic sound began again as Mars' gaze followed the descent of their piece de resistance in home remodeling: a garage door in place of the former front door. The killer difference was that now the whole front half of the house rolled up, revealing the front hall, the parlor, the living room, the stairwell leading upstairs, and Udela's bedroom. Already neighbors were peering out their windows as several more came outside to watch.

Apollo joined Mars. "It's brilliant."

"I know." Mars sighed.

"Apollo?" said Medusa.

Springing, Hermes rejoined them. "I can't wait to see Udela's face the first time someone pushes the doorbell."

"Apollo," said Medusa.

"Yes, Meddles?" said Mars.

"Bite me, Mars," said Medusa.

Mars nudged Apollo. "Just say where."

"You wish, Mar-shall. Apollo."

"Yeah?" Apollo was examining the bruises on his hands.

"Brace yourself," she said, seriously.

Apollo exchanged frowns with his buddies and turned about. "What for?"

And then he saw what for. His eyes popped and his jaw dropped, but only half as far as Mars and Hermes' jaws dropped.

"Look out!" said Hermes. "She's going to pop any second now."

Resembling a bottom heavy duck with a look of bewildered consternation flexing her brows, proud, graceful Athena waddled across the lawn to the picnic table. As soon as she could lay her hand upon the table and rest her weight a little, she looked their way.

Looking quite serious, Venus shadowed her. "You'd better sit down."

"Is that normal?" said Apollo.

Venus shook her head. "Not even for goddesses."

"I knew I should've brought a camera," said Hermes.

Athena frowned suddenly at her great belly. "Ow. Ow. Ow! Quit that."

"What's wrong?" Apollo rushed to her side. He stared at her belly. "Quit what?"

"Ow! Stop kicking me. Apollo!"

"What?"

"Your child is kicking me."

"You in there, stop kicking your mother."

"It figures. It listens to you." Chin tilted high, Athena waddled back inside as briskly as her fertile, engorged body would permit. Before she could reach the back door though – "STOP KICKING ME." She slammed the door behind her.

Venus propped her hands on her hips and fixed her gaze upon Apollo. "Well?"

"Well what?" he said.

"You're just going to stand out here?"

"Well, yes."

Her stare intensified into a glare. "And when Zeus returns, what if he sees her?"

"Oh! Right! Of course."

Stewart and Juliet came strolling down the side-walk just as Apollo slumped toward his back door. They observed Apollo's mood at once.

"Is something wrong, Apollo?" said Juliet.

"Oh, nothing much, but next time I'm wearing a bloody condom." Apollo shut the door hard behind him.

"Okay," said Juliet, as she exchanged odd looks with Stewart.

"Where have you two been?" Hermes fairly hopped up and down in eagerness. "No, wait. Forget that. Do you want to see the surprise we rigged up?"

Stewart shook his head. "Not now." He ushered Juliet ahead of him toward the much abused picnic table.

"What's wrong?" said Venus.

We've been scouring the listings for a place to stay, but everything is beyond our reach," said Juliet.

"How about our house?" said Medusa.

"You don't mean for us to room with you?" said Stewart. "Won't it be crowded?"

"Not after today," said Mars. "We've finished fix-ing up the place and once we finish what we started today, we'll be done."

"And then it's 'Happy Trails', and adios, muchacho," said Hermes.

"So you'll rent the house to us?" said Stewart.

"We're giving it to you – as a wedding present," said Venus. "Right, boys?"

Mars and Hermes nodded at once.

"But I don't want to live next door to your mother, Stewart," said Juliet.

Their bright expressions of delight dimmed almost immediately.

"Don't worry," said Medusa. "We'll sort that out before we leave."

Stewart and Juliet witnessed the wicked, amused little grins that passed between the four deities, and clung a little tighter to each other.

"You aren't going to do anything to them, are you?" said Stewart.

"You mean, aside from what we've done already?" said Hermes.

Firmly, but gently, Venus said, "We won't do anything to them that they won't deserve, Stewart."

"Why doesn't it comfort me to hear that?"

"Because, unlike them, you're a decent person, and you know what all they've done to you and how it felt." Mars walked over and draped his arm over Stewart's shoulders. "Think of us as a long overdue dose of karma. Perhaps when this is all over, they'll have grown consciences. At any rate, they'll be out of your hair by sundown, I promise."

"Has Mum come back yet?" said Stewart.

"Not yet, but – Speak of the devil," said Medusa.

Udela came bustling back. She peered over the fence at them. "You haven't seen Erian have you?"

"No," said Stewart. "Isn't he with you?"

"No." Udela was breathless. "He's run amuck." She glanced up and down the lane, wringing her hands all the while.

Aiken crept outside with his backpack and a suitcase, but he hesitated when he saw Mars, Venus, Hermes, Medusa, and even Stewart and Juliet watching him. At the gate, he froze altogether when he saw his mother staring across at him.

Udela turned sharp again. "What do you think you're doing?"

"Leaving. Where's Erian?" he said after a minute.

Waving her hands and then prodding and shoving, Udela herded Aiken back inside. "Running mad somewhere. Never mind him."

Venus snapped her fingers and bit her lip. "Damn! He was this close to leaving."

Apollo and a restored Athena re-emerged from their own house. Between them, clinging to their hands swung a bright, laughing, five-year-old boy.

Mars gaped. "Where did he come from?"

"You have to ask?" said Athena without a trace of rancor.

"But weren't you still pregnant with him a few minutes ago?" said Mars.

"As you can see, I am no longer pregnant."

Although Venus was quick to stoop down and wave at the little boy, words failed the others.

"This is impossible, isn't it?" said Mars.

"Normally, I would agree," said Apollo, "but having just experienced something of a time warp in there, I think the situation calls for a special arrangement. Hermes, if you would assist us?

"Look! There are a lot of things I'll let you lot bully me into doing, but I'm not a nanny."

"Do you really think we'd entrust our son to you?" said Athena.

"Not if you're going to insult me."

"Enough of that," said Apollo. "Hermes, we need you to escort little Amadeus here to his tutors."

"Amadeus?" said Medusa.

" 'Beloved of God' " – it fits," said Venus. The sunny boy sprang into her arms. She lifted him up. "Why are you sending him away? If you were mine, I'd keep you."

"We'd love nothing more than to keep Amadeus Alarico Benedicto Sandor Candakirana here with us." Athena took on a somber expression.

"Jehosaphat! Why didn't you just name him Fred and keep it simple?" said Hermes.

Apollo sighed. "Because names carry power. His name means 'Beloved of God – Rules All – Blessed – Fierce Rayed – Defender of Man'."

"Ah. Ah. No hair pulling." Venus disentangled her gleaming hair from his eager little fist.

"But he was born and grew to this age in mere minutes, so you can see the problem," said Apollo.

Mars nodded. "In two hours he'll be full grown."

"And making grandparents out of us," said Athena.

Medusa snorted.

Athena looked her dead in the eye. "Seriously."

Medusa's mirth evaporated. "That IS a problem."

Apollo took his son back from Venus. "So we decided that the best thing to do was to slip him into the time stream – which is where we need your swift assistance, Hermes, – so that he would grow up at a normal pace under the care and protection of those who can best teach him what he needs to know."

"Aren't you going to miss him?" said Venus.

Athena took him from Apollo's embrace, saying,

"I am actually, but this is unavoidable."

Mars rubbed his chin. "If Zeus gets so much as a whiff of this kid…"

"He'd devour him. Right," said Hermes.

"We have to hide him from Zeus. If Hermes will serve as messenger between us and our son?" began Athena.

"We'd appreciate it," said Apollo.

Hermes was struck by their plain sincerity. "I'd be glad to do it." He made a face at Amadeus, who giggled and made one back.

The boy stuck out his finger at Mars, and declared, "Funny!"

"He's got you figured out," said Medusa.

"Just to be on the safe side, Hermes, don't take him anywhere near Mt. Olympus," said Mars.

Hermes added earnestly, "I'll be careful."

Athena bounced her son lightly in her embrace, smiling all the while. "If Zeus harms so much as a hair on my son's head, Apollo and I will rip the child out of his belly with our bare hands."

Apollo's eyes flashed. "Let it be clear to anyone who discovers this child's identity that the son of Pajawone Apollo and Pallas Athena shall not be meddled with."

"Right," said Hermes with a salute.

Athena headed toward Hermes, pausing to let Apollo kiss his son, and then handed him over to Hermes.

"Ready to go on a big adventure?" said Hermes.

He looked at his parents and nodded. "Yeah!"

"Then let's go. Where am I taking him?"

Apollo was too overcome to speak.

"To Pythagoras and then to Socrates when he's

nine," said Athena.

Hermes set the boy upon his shoulders. "Say bye-bye."

Amadeus waved both hands. "Bye!"

Making race car noises, Hermes sped off with Amadeus laughing upon his shoulders.

Athena handed Apollo a tissue. "Honestly now."

Apollo wiped his eyes and blew his nose. "I can't help it."

Aiken lurched outside. He backed out, pulling every step of the way on his backpack. "Mum! Let go."

Pulling on the straps, Udela used every ounce of her weight to impede him. "You can't go."

"I can't stay."

"Of course you can. You must."

"I can't and I won't." He yanked his backpack free and tossed it behind him. While Udela chased after it, he lunged inside to haul out his suitcase.

Clutching the backpack, Udela had turned back, but she dropped it to grab hold of his suitcase handle. "Why must you leave?"

"Because SHE..." and he jerked his thumb in Venus' direction, "...has made it impossible for me to stay. I spent half the morning locked up with my barmy brother...and I was there for my own protection because everyone in the whole fucking area wants to KILL me."

"Give them a week. They'll forget all about it."

"Not if I can help it," said Venus.

Udela rushed at the fence. "I told you to stay away from my son."

For a moment Aiken stood forgotten. He snatched up his suitcase and backpack and scuttled toward the gate. He was so busy watching his mother that he didn't see Medusa slip out onto the sidewalk. But when he did look, he saw Medusa holding the gate open for him. Although escape was mere steps away, he froze.

"Oh dear, what has darling Aphrodite done now?" It was Zeus with an indulgent gleam in his eyes, which kindled as they shifted toward Udela.

She lunged toward him at once and seized his arm.

Zeus dropped the grocery bags and closed his arms about her.

Mars sighed. "So much for the eggs." He picked up the bags.

"Come inside and tell me all about it," said Zeus in a bedroom voice. He steered Udela toward her back door.

Medusa made a face.

As keenly as a cat watched a mouse scuttling forth from its hole, Apollo eyed their progress.

Medusa mouthed at Aiken, 'Go on.' She motioned toward the sidewalk. 'Hurry.'

Even Mars stood there gesturing to him. Now Aiken was in a real quandary. Should he trust them? He stood rooted to the spot.

"They have wrecked everything," Udela cried. "Look at the inside of my house. It looks like the inside of a lava lamp. They did that on purpose."

Zeus kept his arm snug about her shoulders and a soothing smile on his face. "Surely it can't be that bad."

"It is! It is! Look for yourself." Udela pushed toward her back door. "Look."

Mildly frustrated, he cast a longing look back at her bedroom window around the corner of the house and said, "Very well." He trod alone through the back door. "Whoa! I haven't seen colors like this since Haight-Ashbury." Then he burst out laughing as his voice receded deeper inside the house.

"I told you so," Udela said, but then she saw Aiken standing near their gate looking back at her.

"Bye, Mum." He turned toward the gate.

"Where do you think you're going?"

"Away. Off to see the world, I guess."

Udela's howl of anger and unhappiness bounced off the rooftops. "What about me?"

"What about you? I'm the one who's the pariah. I'm the one who spent the night in police custody while you spent the night shagging Father Christmas in there."

"I tried to get you out."

"You left Stewart to try to get me and Erian out. You left after only fifteen minutes."

"Did not!"

"Did too!"

"You shouldn't believe what Stewart tells you."

"Evans at the station, remember him? He told me. Stewart merely confirmed what Evans told me."

"When can I expect you back at home?"

"Oh, how about…never?" He waved at her, blew a kiss at Medusa, who looked genuinely startled by his gesture, and set off.

Udela screamed his name long and loudly. Apollo clapped his hands over his ears. Medusa plugged hers. The rest winced and cringed. The horrible din died away with a gasp and a moan.

"Really now!" said Medusa. "I'm sure he'll send you a postcard, Udela."

Udela leaned upon her fencepost and caught her breath. The glance she fixed upon them seethed.

Athena's stare sharpened, but she took on a crooked grin instead.

"What?" said Udela. "You have something to add?"

Athena nodded. "Just this: Erian was telling the truth about us. We are the real Olympians. He isn't crazy."

Udela snorted, but stopped herself. "Stewart, is this true? It can't be."

Stewart thought it interesting how she was taking him seriously all of a sudden. "It is. You'll realize it's true when you really think about everything that's happened."

Udela saw them all anew. "Oh God."

"Oh God, indeed," said Mars. "By the way, guess which discredited deity you were humping last night?"

Udela flailed after the proper outraged response and couldn't find the words. She shook her head as though it would shake away the terrible truth. It was all too much, and even worse, judging by all the neighbors standing in clusters across the street, she had become a spectacle. "I expect you're proud of yourselves."

Apollo nodded. "But prouder still that we've accomplished what we were sent here to do."

"And that would be?" said Udela.

They all gestured to Steward and Juliet.

"They make a lovely couple, wouldn't you agree?" said Venus.

Udela opened her mouth, but she saw the pointlessness of even uttering one more word.

Zeus came back outside. "What were you all on? LSD?"

Casting an odd look at him, Udela shoved past him indoors. "I need a drink and a lie down."

Mars took on a wicked grin. "Wait till she gets an eyeful of her bedroom. She didn't mention it yet, so I don't think she's seen it."

"Whose idea was it to paint it to look like a Hell's

Mouth?" said Zeus.

"Mine. Don't ask," said Mars.

Zeus arched his brow at Mars. "That's my boy."

An outraged howl erupted from Udela's bedroom.

"Another satisfied customer," said Medusa. "Revenge is best served when it's served in fluorescent orange. Should we warn her not to open her bedroom closet?"

Mars said, "Say, 'Dad', why don't you go up and warn her about what's in the closet?"

A chorus of snarling and barking erupted via Udela's bedroom window. Udela shrieked, and they heard a door slam, muffling the raucous baying.

Zeus frowned. "You would have to bring Cerberus here. I had better go in and calm her down. Later, I expect you to remove that fleabag."

"When exactly?" said Apollo.

"Later. Yes, much later." Zeus was smiling to himself. He went in. They heard him bounding upstairs.

Medusa made a face. "He's going to 'calm her down' all right."

Apollo smiled at Mars. "Perfect," both said.

Athena spoke up loud and clear. "Where do you think you are going, Hermes?"

Hermes poked his head up over the fence. "Damn. Have you got eyes in the back of your head?"

Athena turned his way. "Aren't you supposed to be guarding my son?"

"Uh. Yes."

"Then why aren't you with him?"

"Because I'm here."

Apollo stepped between Athena and Hermes. "Something happened, or you wouldn't be skulking around here. Where is our son?"

"I can tell you where he is not," said Hermes.

"Go on," said Apollo.

"He is NOT with Pythagoras any longer."

Apollo could be as patient as a saint sometimes. "Then where is he?"

"He's nowhere near Mt. Olympus, if that's what you're worried about."

Apollo growled, "Hermes."

Hermes rolled his eyes as though stating the obvious. "He's with Siddhartha at Bodh Gaya."

Athena took on a look of pleasant astonishment. "Well, I can't think of a better place for him to be."

Full of longing, Hermes eyed their back door, but between Apollo's stare and also the manner in which the Sun God folded his hands across his chest, he didn't dare move another inch.

"Now, you cattle rustler, why isn't my son still with my great protégé Pythagoras?" said Apollo.

Hermes' sudden grin was not a good sign. "There was an incident."

"An incident?" Apollo arched his brow.

"The kid was hungry."

"What did you do?" said Athena.

"Do? What makes you think I did anything?" Hermes managed a nervous half-laugh.

"Because we know you," said Mars.

"You'd better tell them before they turn you into a carrier pigeon, Hermes," said Medusa.

"He wanted a burrito, so I went and got him one."

Apollo looked appalled. "Not with beans?"

"There was some beef in it too." Hermes grinned and shrugged. "Needless to say, the boy was banished."

"But of course!" Apollo covered his face in his hands and half-groaned and half-laughed. He uncovered

his face. "Pythagoras was vegetarian. He absolutely for-
bade his followers from eating meat and beans. Rather
than flee through a bean field and desecrate themselves
followers of his have died. Didn't you know that?"

Hermes stuck his finger in the corner of his mouth
and grinned. "Oops."

"Oops? My bloody ass – oops! No, your bloody
ass, Hermes, when I get my hands on you." Apollo began to roll up his sleeves.

Hermes shook his finger at him. "Don't you wish
you had the time, Apollo?"

"What do you mean?"

Hermes drew out a pocket watch and consulted it.
"The boy's scheduled to go to Eton in five minutes.
He'll miss his entire first year, IF I don't go get him now.
The choice is yours: Either I stay here, and you can
thrash me soundly, or I can light out for India to fetch
your boy."

Apollo glanced toward the Dunk household. A
familiar telltale rhythmic bumping had begun.

Medusa looked nauseated. "Predictable. That
Zeus has a one track mind."

Apollo took on a sharp grin, which he shared with
Mars. "I will go get my son."

"You will go get Hera," said Mars.

Hermes impudent grin vanished. "Huh?"

"You heard me," said Mars.

"Go get the 'Big Gun'," said Apollo.

"Whatever for?"

"Because Stewart and Juliet here cannot possibly
be expected to live next door to Udela," said Mars.

"I'd prefer not to," said Juliet lowly, tearing her
distracted gaze from Udela's bedroom window. Once
again, she and Stewart clung to each other amid their po-

tent and mercurial neighbors.

"This time let's see if we can't get rid of two birds with one, big, mean rock," said Apollo.

Hermes looked Mars in the eyes. "Are you sure about this? You know what she can be like."

Mars narrowed his gaze at Udela's bedroom window. "Get the 'Big Gun'."

"Yes, sir." Hermes saluted him and set off at a steady march.

"I'll check on the boy." Apollo kissed Athena on the cheek and left even more briskly than Hermes had.

"What's going to happen?" said Stewart.

"Justice," said Athena. "At long last, justice."

"At any rate," said Mars, as he slapped the couple on the shoulders, "Udela will never darken your doorstep ever again. That I can guarantee."

Stewart met Mars's glance. "She isn't going to be turned into a slug, is she? I mean, no one deserves that, not even my horrible selfish slag of a mum."

Athena shrugged. "Frankly, I'm hoping that Zeus will get the slug treatment."

"He has certainly earned it," said Medusa.

"Then let's hope that that self-empowerment seminar Artemis took her to actually did her some good," said Mars. "Still, when she shows up - and she WILL show up – you both might want to hide inside."

"Whatever you say," said Stewart.

"Perhaps we should go in and have a look around," said Juliet. "It is going to be our home now after all."

Stewart frowned at the cloudbank darkening the southern horizon. "Let's." He ushered her inside very quickly.

Hermes returned and leaned against their gatepost.

"Where's Hera?" said Mars.

"She didn't believe me about her little doggie being missing. She went to check first."

"Where's Apollo?" said Athena.

"He had to stay behind to keep an eye on the boy. He's a spirited lad that son of yours."

"Why don't I like the sound of that?" said Athena.

Hermes rolled his eyes. "Don't get your robes all bunched up. The boy IS thirteen now."

"And you know how teenagers can be," said Mars with arched brows.

"Actually, it isn't that he's wayward or overly rambunctious. It's just that…Well … Look at who his parents are. The child of Athena and Apollo was bound to be precocious, and like his mother, he doesn't suffer fools gladly."

Athena scrunched her eyes closed. "All right. Tell me what happened."

Medusa looked off to the south. "Was that thunder?" she muttered.

Stewart crept back outside, eyeing the sky.

Juliet shadowed him. "What's wrong?"

"Can't you feel it?" he said. "The air feels heavy."

Hermes was enjoying Athena's consternation. "Well, put it this way. The school bullies are afraid to so much as look cross-eyed at him, especially after he turned the headmaster into a Texas Horned Toad."

"So that's why Apollo stayed behind in the time stream," said Athena.

Only moderately sympathetic, Hermes nodded. "The boy needs a little fatherly guidance just now – what with all the girls taking an interest in him and so forth."

Venus' eyes went wide. She pressed her hand to her bosom. "I don't even want to think about what

Apollo could be telling him."

Hermes frowned at the erratic sounds of piggy de-light coming from Udela's bedchamber. Then his gaze settled upon Juliet and Stewart, who watched everything in an awed, mute kind of silence, rather akin to two mice amid a herd of buffalo. They were just hoping that they wouldn't get trampled in the chaos. He called over to them, "So, have you two decided to accept our gift?"

"What gift?" said Stewart.

"This house, space cadet."

"I'm not wild about the idea of living next door to Udela," said Juliet.

"Me either," said Stewart.

"Honestly, I don't think she's going to want to live here much longer," said Medusa. Eyeing the sky, she edged closer to Stewart and Juliet.

Apollo sauntered back.

"How's our son?" said Athena.

"Everything's fine. We had a nice long talk about personal responsibility and the true nature of conse-quences. He got the point."

"Are you sure?" said Athena.

"Well, I told him that if he acted up again, you would be the one to visit. He promised to be good, so I came back. Did I miss anything?"

"All we need is…," said Venus.

"All right! Where is my dog?!"

Hera.

Yes, indeed. Hera. It was the Big Gun herself, looking better than she had since 200 AD in her new couture outfit and hairdo. Ares' stressed old Frau of a mother had vanished. In her place strode a refreshed earth mother dressed in the height of La Dolce Vita glamour, complete with a tight, slit skirt, high heels, a silk

wrap carelessly tied about her shoulders, and her dark,
dark brunette hair arranged in a high elegant hive. She
removed her cats-eye shaped sunglasses and leveled
fierce eyes upon them. "Hermes said that Zeus had
taken my dog for a walk. He knows not to do that without my permission. Where is my baby?"

Somewhat dazzled, Apollo inclined his head a little. "Milady Hera, how was the seminar?"

Hera's expression turned thoughtful. "Good actually. I'm glad your sister talked me into going."

"It helped then?" said Athena.

"It gave me a whole new perspective on everything."

"Everything?" said Mars.

"Everything," said Hera.

Leaning close to Stewart, Juliet whispered.
"Who's that?"

Stewart looked petrified. It took him a moment to
respond. "That is none other than Hera, Zeus's wife and
queen."

"Uh oh."

"No kidding," said Stewart with a glance at his
mother's window. "This is going to get blisteringly ugly."

They clung to each other's hands.

"So where's my dog?" Hera demanded.

"Zeus still has it," said Hermes.

"Cerberus is my baby. He hates Cerberus." She
stopped ranting a moment to prop her hands on her hips
and cock her head at Hermes. "Why do I get the feeling
that you had something to do with this?"

Hermes gave her a big smile as he stepped around
Mars. "Whatever I did, HE put me up to it."

Hera's formidable glance shifted to her son.
"Ares?"

"Cerberus is perfectly fine. We didn't harm a hair on any of his three heads."

"But you know how much Zeus hates my dog. He hid under my bed for a week because Zeus threw a sandal at him."

"Well, Mother, Cerberus is in the house next door." Mars nodded toward the Dunks' place.

"Why?"

"Think of this as a test," said Apollo.

Hera cocked her brow at the golden one. "A test?"

"To see how much you absorbed from that seminar," said Athena.

"Come on!" Venus shook her fist in the air. "Grrrrl power."

"And all you have to do is ring the doorbell," said Mars.

"And I'll get my dog back?" said Hera.

"And your self-respect too," muttered Apollo.

"Among other things," Medusa whispered back.

Frowning, Hera strode toward the Dunks' front door. Upstairs, things were reaching a prolonged crisis. Hera noticed the many neighbors watching, but she was more concerned about the fate of her overgrown three-headed puppy than she was curious about so many gawkers.

Hermes lunged over to the gaping gate and peered round for a look. Medusa, Athena, and Venus crossed their fingers. There ensued a brief, but ominous silence, followed by a doorbell, which resounded up and down the lane with wincing clarity.

"This is going to be good," said Mars.

Amid the sudden, immediate sounds of the whole front of the house ascending rose also the horrified howl of Udela Dunk, the startled curses that blasted forth from Zeus' lips, and Cerberus' plaintive howling chorus the instant he sensed that his Mummy was nigh.

Stewart and Juliet rushed to the gate.

"Oh – my – God," said Stewart.

"Look!" shouted a neighbor. "Udela's shagging Father Christmas."

"Ewww," chorused the neighbors, or at least those who weren't pointing and laughing, or filming the tangled couple thrashing about on the scorching neon red bed.

"You son of a bitch!" shouted Hera. "I can't leave you alone for two days together without you running off and humping some slut."

Cerberus howled and clawed on the closet door. It rattled ominously on its hinges.

Hera launched herself upstairs as the front of the house descended in place again.

"It wasn't what you think. She seduced me," Zeus shouted as the garage door closed.

"Actually," commented Venus, "for once he's telling the truth."

"Ah, irony," said Apollo with a beatific smile.

"Damn it! Now I can't hear what they're saying...or see what's happening." Hermes darted out and rang the doorbell again and again up went the front half of her house. He came back smiling. "This is great!"

Medusa glanced up and down the street. "I think the new door is going to be popular with the neighborhood kids."

Hermes giggled.

Still spilling out of her clothes, Udela rushed outside. The neighbors hooted and cheered. Every wife she had wronged laughed and jeered at her. Every straying husband she had bedded laughed.

Behind her, the whole house shook on its foundations.

"But Dear…"

"Don't you 'Dear' me. Artemis was right, Zeus. You are a total slut."

"A man can't be a slut."

"Yes, he can, and you're the poster boy proof of that."

The garage door closed again, leaving Udela stranded outside cringing under her neighbors' stares and laughter.

"A man has needs."

"Needs? Needs? Let me tell you what you need: pack your things and get the hell out of Olympus. No! Don't even bother to show your miserable, sodding face at home. Chiron will bring your junk to you."

"Where will I go?"

"I don't care. Just get out of my sight and take that underdressed sausage with you."

"Wait. Wait. Don't turn that monster loose."

"You have until the count of three. One…"

Cerberus snarled and clawed at the closet door. Even the outer walls shook.

"…Two…"

"I'm going!" Zeus threw open the garage door with one mighty, panicked heave.

"THREE!" Hera shouted triumphantly.

Cerberus bounded downstairs. The neighbors screamed and ducked inside their own homes.

"Shit!" Zeus grabbed Udela, or rather, she latched onto him in a panic and he was too panic-stricken himself to bother to shake her loose, as he caught a fortuitous whirlwind and vaulted across the sky, heading west.

Hermes did a victory dance.

"Mars, you're a genius," said Athena.

"Wow. Thank you, Athena," he replied. He held out a set of keys and jingled them. "The offer still stands, son. Are you ready to move in?"

Stewart snatched them. "I sure am."

"Excellent decision." He tousled Stewart's hair and slapped him on the shoulders.

"Ow."

"Sorry. I forget my own strength sometimes."

"No, it's fine." Stewart met Juliet's smiling gaze. "Everything's fine, isn't it?"

Juliet nodded and rushed into his embrace.

"What shall I do with the old house now?" said Stewart.

"Sell tickets," said Hermes.

"Give it to Erian. You'll find him hiding out at Stevens' pub when you decide to go looking for him, if you decide to go looking for him. He'll come back eventually," said Athena with a shrug.

With Zeus long gone, Cerberus, that mutant Rottweiler, bounced about on the sidewalk before Hera wagging so hard his whole enormous body wriggled. The monstrous hound's six eyes sparkled. All three heads yapped.

"That's my good boy." Hera stoked his heads, each one as they vied to be foremost for her attention. Taking out her leash, she fastened it to his harness. "Let's go home, baby." She gazed at Mars. " 'Coming home for supper tonight? I'll make your favorite risotto."

They all looked at him.

Mars shrugged. "Sure, I haven't been there in ages, so I might as well pop round," he said. "See you then."

Still baby-talking to Cerberus, Hera strolled down the sidewalk. The locals scattered in terror.

Apollo kept glancing at his watch.

"Why do you keep looking at your watch?" said Athena.

"Because if we don't leave shortly, we're going to miss it."

"Miss what?" said Mars.

"Our boy is graduating and we should be there. Right, Athena?"

"Yes, of course." She headed toward him.

"Besides, I need you there to help talk some sense into him."

Athena's steps faltered. "Oh?"

"No, it's nothing terrible. He was talking about going to Yale or Harvard."

"Over my dead body! He's going to either Oxford or Cambridge. Or it's the French Foreign Legion for him."

Apollo took her by the arm. "That's why we both need to be there: to talk some sense into him. We'd better hurry."

"Right." Athena looked back, smiled and gave a little wave. "Bye."

Stewart and Juliet waved back.

Venus followed. "I think I'd like to see how 'little' Amadeus turned out." She blew a little kiss and waved at Stewart and Juliet as she strolled after Athena and Apollo.

"Venus darling?" said Apollo.

"Yes, Apollo sweetie?" she replied.

"Keep your mitts off my son."

"Oh, you're no fun."

"I mean it."

Venus sighed. "Killjoy."

Medusa shook Stewart and Juliet's hands. "Have a good life, you two." Then she sprinted off. "Wait up, Venus."

"Coming, Mars?" said Hermes.

"In a moment. There's one last thing."

Mars went around the side of the house and came back with the gate. Simply and efficiently he set the re-painted gate in place, put the pins in place and, stepping out, closed it behind him. "There. Finished."

"Thank you," said Juliet.

"It just needed fixing. That's all. Take care, you two."

Mars shook Stewart's hand and gave Juliet a friendly kiss on the cheek. Hermes lunged toward Juliet, but Mars caught him and steered him ahead.

"No, you don't, troublemaker," said Mars.

"Spoilsport," groused Hermes.

"You can have 'fun' at the graduation."

"Ohh. Right!" Hermes looked back and waved with both arms, then trotted off alongside Mars.

Ominously, the words – 'comely female co-eds' came from Hermes' lips as he, Mars, and the rest van-ished beneath the blue shadow of a passing cloud. The lane stood peaceful again, populated only by humble, if slightly shell-shocked mortals going about their lives.

Appreciating what a beautiful day it was, especially once the dust had settled, Stewart and Juliet embraced.

The End